HIS NEW JAM

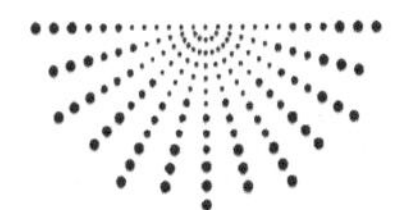

SHANNYN SCHROEDER

ACKNOWLEDGMENTS

Each book I write requires research. Sometimes, I can sit at my computer and Google everything. Other times, I need to reach out to actual people. I know nothing about music (other than I like to listen to it) and even less about marching band. My own kids were a pretty good resource when it came to understanding music lessons. It's good to know they learned something. I want to thank Ryann Murphy and her friend Amy Mackey, who both shared their college marching band experiences with me. I used what they offered, but any mistakes are all my own. There's a world of talented musicians out there, so I also want to thank all the musicians who put their videos up on YouTube for me to learn from.

CHAPTER ONE

Sydney shoved another spoonful of cereal into her mouth and stared at the calendar. Two weeks. That's all she had left to suffer through until marching band was over for the year. Two weeks of practice and drills and football games. Then she could pack up the fucking cymbals until next summer.

Her older sister, Trisha, came into the kitchen still in her robe. "Aren't you going to be late?"

"Whatever." Sydney slurped at her milk to prevent Trish from nagging again. They were both well aware she needed the scholarship the marching band gave her for school. It didn't mean Syd had to like it.

"I don't see what's so bad about band. You get to play the instrument you love. The music's not all bad. So the uniforms are a little dorky, but you look good on the field." Trisha poured herself a cup of coffee.

"I don't get to play the instrument I love. I play the damn cymbals. Just once I would like to be given an actual drum. I sucked it up last year as the new kid, waiting, thinking that at some point, as guys graduate, I could step up. Instead, it's this patronizing attitude. The drums are heavy. They'll be awkward. There are already other players waiting. But the worst is that I'm so good at the cymbals, they don't want to lose me." She dumped her bowl in the sink. "It's all bullshit. I don't even know why I need to finish school. I want to play. I don't need a degree to do that."

Trisha sighed the same way their mom always had. "We made a deal with Dad. You get to live with me in the city as long as you're in school."

"That was when I was underage. I'm twenty-one. I can live wherever I want."

Trish patted her arm. "But you don't want to let Dad down. Suck it up. Only another year and a half until graduation. Only a few weeks until you can forget about band for a while."

It annoyed her how well her sister knew her. Of course she wouldn't let their dad down. He'd decided the only way for them to have a good life was to go to college, as if college could solve every problem. He held fast to the idea that if he had gone to college, his life, and by extension their lives, would've been so much easier.

So she was in school, getting a graphic design degree that would be useless because all she wanted to do was play music. Real music, rock, with a band, for an audience that wanted to hear it.

But Trish did have a point: Only a few weeks and she could say good-bye to being out in the cold, stomping on hard grass, pretending to enjoy herself during a football game. She tossed her backpack into her car and drove to the field. She shoved a hat on her head and grabbed her cymbals from the trunk. Just as she slammed the lid down, someone whistled at her.

Sydney's head popped up, ready to berate whatever asshole thought it was okay to catcall, when she saw her friend Emma running down the aisle of cars. She skidded to a halt in front of Sydney. "Whoa. You look ready to bite someone's head off."

"I thought you were some guy whistling at me."

"Lighten up. So what if I was? You look ready to commit bodily harm."

"I'm just extra cranky. It's cold and I want the season to be over. Plus, it's a new week, so that tenor hasn't done his shit yet."

"What?"

"You know who I'm talking about. The tenor sax guy who hits on anything female. Every week since the summer, I can't walk by without him playing some song at me."

Emma smirked. "How do you know he's playing for you?"

They headed toward the field together. "He stands off to the side and waits for me to get within ten feet before playing a note. Trust me, he's flirting, in his own lame way."

Emma nudged her shoulder. "His name is Hunter. He's a huge flirt, but totally harmless. He's having fun. He does it to make people smile. No one takes him seriously. As far as I know, he's never dated anyone from band. Plus, he's cute."

Emma had her there. The guy was cute, but even Syd knew he had a reputation for dating around a lot. She hadn't given him too much thought. Okay, that was a lie. Last season she crushed on him pretty hard, but he hadn't given her a second glance. She had no idea what had changed, but these past few months had been torturous.

She had no desire to waste her time on a fling with some guy who would toss her aside next week. "Does anyone ever flirt back? Maybe that's why he doesn't date anyone."

"Oh, no, plenty flirt back. It's a game to keep things fun. How could you not have caught on?"

"It wasn't included in band camp." Sydney wasn't quite sure what to do with that. They neared the mob of people that would turn into organized rows of musicians. Sure enough, Tenor Guy stood off to the side, staring in her direction even as he carried on a conversation with another sax player.

He said nothing as he brought his instrument up and played the first notes. Syd continued walking, trying to ignore him. She got a few feet past him when the notes of his song bounced through her mind and recognition hit. He was playing the damn Disney song, "Let It Go."

Oh, yeah, this guy was hilarious. So he thought she was an ice queen. He got close to the chorus and Syd paused mid-stride. Just as the ice queen accepted her fate, Sydney clashed her cymbals together and winked over her shoulder at Hunter. She was fine with being cold.

∼

HOLY SHIT. HUNTER BLINKED AND ALMOST MISSED A note. Not only did Sydney Peters turn around and acknowledge that he was playing a song for her, she actually winked at him. Sure, it was more of a fuck-you wink than a flirtatious one, but it was still progress. He'd tried everything since summer to get her to react. The Pink Panther song didn't get her; neither did "Happy" or "Call Me Maybe." Although he thought he'd gotten an eye roll for that last one.

He liked to flirt with the band members. It kept things interesting when they spent a bunch of time marching and getting yelled at. It never went anywhere beyond fun conversation. There was something about Sydney that made him relentless. She always looked borderline miserable coming to practice. He thought maybe she wasn't a morning person, but even at games she looked irritated, like she'd rather be anywhere else than on the field.

She didn't talk to many people, except Emma. Emma was nice. For a trumpet player. But Sydney didn't strike him as nice, which made him want to poke at her. It had taken a long time, but he'd finally gotten a reaction.

He liked that wink so much he might reconsider his rule against dating a band member. He'd love to get her alone to see if she continued to be distant and edgy. It was his last season of band, which was almost over, and he'd graduate in the spring. Maybe it was time to lift the ban on band members.

Practice was starting, so Hunter ran to get into place. While they gathered in formation to practice the drill, he couldn't help but smile.

Two hours later, practice ended and his fingers were numb. He should've gone to school somewhere in the South. He looked at the drum line to find Sydney, but he didn't see her face. Then he saw her on the outskirts of the group, edging away. Hunter took a step in her direction.

"Hey, Peters," the drum major called.

Her head snapped up.

"Practice room at two o'clock. We need to run through this again."

Although her jaw clenched, she offered a sharp nod. Then she turned and hustled downfield. Approaching her now wouldn't be smart. He wasn't even sure what he'd say. But he got out of class at two thirty, so maybe he'd wander on down to the practice rooms to bump into her.

"Hey, Hunter," Mike called. He was another tenor, and they sometimes hung out, but Hunter wouldn't call them friends. "You having a party for New Year's again?"

"You know it."

"Can I bring a friend?"

"Don't see why not." Hunter put his sax into the case. "I'll text you details later. I need to talk to my roommate about it."

"Cool. See you Wednesday."

Hours later, Hunter had walked past music practice rooms and had no luck finding Sydney. He checked the time. He was supposed to meet Adam and Free at the comic shop at three thirty. If he didn't head out soon, he'd be late.

He hit the last hallway of practice rooms. It figured the drummers would take the biggest rooms in the farthest building. As he clomped down the stairs, Daniel—not Dan or Danny—the drum major, came out of a room. When no one followed, Hunter thought he'd missed her.

Until a slow beat came from the room where Daniel had left. He stood outside the room and listened for a minute. Then he recognized the tune, the same one he'd played to Sydney this morning. He silently opened the door and entered. She noticed him immediately and shot him a dirty look, but didn't stop playing.

Hunter took a seat at another set of drums and picked up where she played. Her eyes narrowed as she watched him. She picked up the tempo and he followed. She ramped it up again.

Now it just felt like a competition.

He kept up with her—barely. She was good, and he wasn't sure why that kind of surprised him, but it did.

When the song ended, he stood and set the sticks on the stool. "Remind me to never go up against you in any kind of battle. You're relentless."

"You're one to talk."

He smiled. "Seriously. You're good."

"You're not bad yourself. For a reed sucker."

He let the playful insult roll off him. "So what are you pissed off about?"

"Who said I'm pissed?"

"Your face."

"Maybe I just have a resting bitch face."

He laughed. He couldn't help it. She was funny without trying. "Nah. I've seen the resting bitch face." With his index finger he circled the air in front of her head. "This is pissed off. My guess is Daniel said something."

"Daniel's always saying something." She stood and tucked her sticks in her backpack.

Hunter knew he was about to lose her. "Can I ask you a question?"

The corner of her mouth lifted. "You just did."

"Why do you hate band?"

"Because it sucks. It's boring. And I will forever be relegated to playing the cymbals, even though I play as well as, if not better than, at least half the drum line."

Ahhh…now it made sense. Those guys tended to be a little full of themselves. "So why do it?"

"It pays the bills."

"Huh?"

"Scholarship." She hoisted her bag onto her shoulder and headed for the door.

"See you at practice Wednesday?"

"As if I have a choice?"

She sounded so miserable he wanted to cheer her up. "I take requests."

"What?" she asked with her hand on the doorknob.

"You seemed to like 'Let It Go.' I take requests. Something you want to hear?"

She turned and leaned against the door. "Are you saying that if I name a song, you're going to go home and learn it just to play it for me at practice on Wednesday?"

Not exactly. He was thinking more like a song for next week, but she was issuing a challenge. "Sure."

She tilted her head up and narrowed her eyes

again as she studied the ceiling for inspiration. When her gaze returned to his, she smiled wickedly, and he knew he was in trouble.

"'Sweet Child O' Mine.'"

He stared at her.

"Guns N' Roses. See you Wednesday, Tenor." Then she slipped out the door before he could form a response.

He knew the song, but it wasn't one he'd ever considered playing with his sax. His drums? Sure. His guitar? Even better. His night just became full.

He checked his watch. If he sped all the way to the comic shop, he might make it on time. Barely. Catching crap from his friends for being late in order to make real contact with Sydney was well worth it.

When he pulled up at the shop, he was late, so he rushed through the door. Free and Adam were standing at the counter. "Why did I have to come here if we're just talking about the New Year's Eve party? Couldn't we do this at home later?"

"Free has to meet Cary at the gym."

"Then I have rehearsal," Free added.

"Why couldn't it wait? We have, like, a month before the party." He'd avoided this conversation because he had a feeling he knew what it was about.

Free straightened. "We need to talk about invitations. We don't want a repeat of last year."

"Why not? Last year was epic."

Adam crossed his arms. "Your word-of-mouth campaign led to an apartment full of strangers."

"They weren't all strangers."

"Just the entire marching band."

"Not all of the band came, and it was fun." The drum line missed out, as usual, and only half the brass showed.

"Except for all the drunk bodies laying all over the place the following morning."

Free held up his hands. "I can't say much about that since I don't live with you guys and therefore don't suffer those repercussions, but I agree that it was too crowded to actually have fun with friends."

Adam pointed at Hunter. "And don't forget the catfight that broke out."

"That wasn't my fault. I'm irresistible." In truth, having two girls brawl because they each thought he somehow *belonged* to her hadn't been as cool as it sounded.

If he left it up to Free and Adam, the entire party would consist of the three of them and maybe five other people sitting around sharing a case of beer. His friends needed help, and he'd always taken it upon himself to make it happen. In a flash, he knew how to get them to agree to a bigger party.

Hunter's gaze bounced between his friends. "Does that mean you guys are going to have dates this year?"

"Nope," Adam answered, and Free dodged him.

Hunter sighed, even though it was the answer he'd expected. "You guys are pitiful. The epitome of nerds. You get dates, I won't tell everyone and their cousin to come to our party."

He knew the chances of that happening were slim. He'd have his blowout party. Besides, the more people he invited, the greater *their* odds were for hooking up with someone.

"You have a date?" Free asked.

He thought of Sydney, who shouldn't even be in the running. "Not yet. I have plenty of time. Working on some options."

And just like that, Sydney became a real option. He didn't know why he was willing to toss out his no-band-members rule for her, but he knew he wanted a chance.

The door opened behind him and Adam greeted the customer by name, but something about Adam's face made Hunter turn to look. A girl with dark hair stared at them with wide eyes before turning to look at comics. Hunter waved a hand toward the girl.

"What?" Adam whispered.

"Ask her, you idiot. She's cute."

"She's not like that."

Hunter shook his head. Adam needed more help than he'd thought. "Every girl is dateable."

Adam didn't respond. At the rate he moved, Hunter had no worries about the size of their party.

CHAPTER TWO

*W*ednesday morning was bitter cold and Sydney was late heading to practice. As she raced across the field, she hadn't even given Hunter a thought, until someone suddenly started playing "Sweet Child O' Mine." It was a little rough, but she'd recognize the music anywhere. She glanced over her shoulder and saw Hunter leave formation to follow her. If he hadn't been section leader, he would've gotten in trouble.

As she neared the drum line, Daniel stepped forward and said, "Are you done playing with your boyfriend so we can get to work?"

She felt her face go fifty shades of red. The brass section snickered, which she clearly heard because Hunter had stopped playing. With her head down, she rushed to her spot.

"Hey, man, cut her some slack. We haven't started yet. I'm just having some fun."

Sydney's mouth dried. Now *everyone* stared, wondering what was going on. She wanted to tell Hunter to go away, that she didn't need him to defend her, but the damage was already done. Anything she said would only make it worse.

"Have fun on your own time."

Hunter stepped closer and although she couldn't hear what he said, she knew it couldn't be good. Heated words were exchanged and the crowd around her seemed to lean forward en masse to hear. Not her. She didn't want to know. She wanted to slink away without being noticed.

Then Hunter stepped back, pointed at her, and said loud enough for everyone to hear, "You don't even know how good she is because your head is so far up your ass."

"You run your section your way. Leave my people to me."

Oh God. Her stomach revolted and her Cheerios threatened a return trip. The bandleader called everyone to their spots, forcing Hunter and Daniel apart. He eyed the two of them, but didn't ask questions. As he took his place, Daniel glared at her. He didn't like being questioned. She'd learned that early on. All she wanted to do was keep her head down and finish school.

Practice was a mess. She couldn't stop thinking about Hunter, and not in a good way. Why the hell had he said anything? When she told him to play "Sweet Child O' Mine," she figured he'd give up. Having him actually play it, knowing he learned it for her, made her warm and tingly. But sticking his nose in the drum line pissed her off. Now everyone thought they were together.

That she was one of his girls who couldn't help but fall for him.

Ha! Fat chance of that happening. She'd

learned her lesson about guys like him. She'd already lost too much time trying to fix her life and create a new reputation for herself.

She might not be seen as the campus sweetheart, but she also wouldn't be considered the band slut.

As soon as practice ended, she ran off the field. Daniel would most likely want an additional practice today, especially since she was off beat several times. She knew the drill and the music, but she'd been flustered by the whole scene with Hunter. She'd be better off practicing alone.

She needed to blow off steam, and she had an hour until class. Moving straight to the practice rooms, she hoped, since it was still early, that she'd find an empty space. She ducked into the first free room with a drum set and sat down. After a quick warm-up, she slid right into one of her favorite songs: "Bad Reputation."

Halfway through, the door swung open. She hadn't checked the sign-up, so a sinking feeling hit her that she might have to leave. But Hunter strode through the door, an easy smile creasing his face.

She wanted to jab him with her drumstick. How could he smile at her like that after the trouble he'd caused? She fought the urge to throw a stick at him and continued to play. By the time she'd finished, her muscles were warm and her jaw hurt from being clenched.

Hunter stayed, leaning against the door, watching her every movement.

"What do you want?" she asked as she reached into her bag for a bottle of water.

"I wanted to make sure you were okay. You looked upset after practice."

"I'm fine."

He studied her face while she gulped water.

"No you're not. You're pissed again."

She glared at him.

"What did I do?"

She pressed her toes into the floor to stop herself from running at him. "I don't need you defending me to Daniel or anyone else."

"Daniel's a prick. I was trying to get him to lighten up."

"Then why bring me into it at all? You singled me out in front of everyone."

"You said yourself he never gives you a chance."

He stepped away from the door. If he had any inkling of the anger vibrating through her, he offered no sign. He sauntered closer, like he didn't have a care in the world.

"First, it's not your problem. Second, did you really think *you* could change anything?"

He shrugged, which infuriated her more. He liked to stir up trouble and sit back and watch.

"Go away, Tenor."

"Hunter. My name's Hunter."

She knew but didn't want to care. He was within touching range now, and the tension between them was palpable. She raised an eyebrow to convey her indifference as she tried to ignore the electrified air bouncing between them.

"I have a favor to ask."

"Your timing sucks."

"You're not the first person to say that." He

turned a huge grin on her. "In my defense, I was trying to be nice out there, not piss you off."

She grunted at him, determined not to be swayed by the smile.

"I want you to teach me to play drums." He fingered the edge of the floor tom.

"You know how to play. I've heard you."

"I can wing it. I have a good ear, but I want to be able to really play."

"I'm no teacher." She gulped the rest of her water. She'd never thought about lessons, but it might be a way to make money.

"But you're good."

"So is everyone else on the drum line."

"But I like you."

She snorted. "You like everyone."

There was the careless shrug again. "You in?"

"What's in it for me?"

He leaned over the crash cymbal. "What do you want?"

He asked like it was a dirty little secret and it made her blood rush in ways it shouldn't. She couldn't afford to be attracted to someone like him, someone who wanted all the attention on him, someone who would make everyone stare at her like he had this morning.

"Nothing from you."

He rocked back on his heels and nodded his head slowly. "How about a paying gig?"

"You're going to pay me to teach you?"

"No. But my band has a regular gig on the weekends and my drummer is going home for the holidays. Unless you're going somewhere?"

Her resolve to avoid Hunter began to dissolve

like ice under rock salt. He offered the one thing she needed: experience with a band. She'd failed at putting together her own band numerous times, mostly because she expected too much from people or she rubbed them the wrong way.

She bit her lip. If she took this deal, she would be spending her entire break with Hunter. They would have band practice together and private lessons and work on the weekends. Hitching her chin up, she asked, "What kind of music?"

"Mostly covers of classic rock."

Her heart sped. It seemed too good to be true. "How often does your band practice and how many lessons are you looking for?"

He started to shrug, but then seemed to think better of it. "My guy, Kevin, won't be leaving until after finals, but I think you should jump in early, if it suits your schedule. We usually practice two or three days a week." The corner of his mouth flicked up again. "I'm ready to start lessons immediately."

"I need to think about it. I'll let you know."

"Okay. Don't take too long, though. I'm gonna need a replacement for Kevin."

Then he spun on his heel and walked out. Sydney released air from deep in her lungs. Something about that guy did things to her and she didn't like it. Flirting with him on the field had been a mistake. She saw that now, regardless of what Emma had said. What would happen if she agreed to spend more time with him? Rumors would definitely start flying.

She slung her bag over her shoulder to go to

class. Hunter had already taken up enough space in her head for one day.

~

Hunter walked into the apartment near midnight. "Adam?" No response. Where the hell could Adam be? It wasn't like he had a social life. Hunter had just gotten off from a night at Andy's Jazz Club. He loved playing there more than anything, so when he was asked to work an extra night tomorrow to fill in, he jumped at the chance. Great musicians surrounded him there, and he always learned something new. The passion they displayed had made him think of Sydney in the practice room.

He flipped on lights as he walked through the apartment and went to the kitchen. He kicked off his shoes under the table before reaching into the cabinet for some cereal. He shook the box. Damn, it was light. If he ate this now, he wouldn't have enough for breakfast. Then again, if he slept in, he wouldn't need breakfast. Satisfied with his decision, he sat at the table and scooped a handful of cereal into his mouth. A few flakes hit the table.

The front door opened and closed. "Hey," Hunter called.

A minute later, Adam stood behind him. "At least you're not spilling on the floor this time. Why can't you make a bowl like a normal person?"

"Then I'd have to clean the bowl. This way, I don't dirty anything."

Adam rolled his eyes and reached into the refrigerator for a beer. He held one out to Hunter.

Hunter accepted it, even though he wasn't really in the mood for one. If Adam was offering, something was up. "Where were you tonight?" he asked as he popped the top on the beer.

Adam sank into the chair across from him. "Reese's apartment working on the comics."

Hunter sighed. "So you had a whole night alone with a cute girl and you drew pictures."

"And watched *Thor.*"

"That's progress, I suppose."

"No progress. We're just friends."

Hunter leaned forward and studied his roommate "You act like you're just friends. You keep saying that, but that's not what you want. Did she shoot you down?"

"What? No. We're working together. That's it."

"So that explains why you're so wound up you need to have a beer after being alone with her."

"Look. Reese is cute. I'll give you that. But I'm not into her."

Hunter slugged back some beer, not enjoying the taste mixed with sugary cereal one bit. "Then you won't care if I ask her out."

"You can't go out with her."

"Why not? She's cute and you don't want her."

"Because it'd be weird. You going out with my friend. What if she slept over with you? No."

The look of fear on Adam's face was worth playing this out. "I can keep it simple. We'll go back to her place."

"I'll be stuck in the middle of a mess when you dump her."

"Who says I'll dump her? Maybe she's the

woman to tame me." Okay, maybe he'd taken it too far.

Adam snorted. "How much have you had to drink? This can't be your first beer."

"It is." He pointed a finger at Adam. "I'm excellent at getting them to break up with me."

"Fuck you. I don't want her pissed off at me because of something you did."

Adam held back pretty well, but Hunter knew his friend. He just needed to press the right button to get him to admit it. "I'll invite her to the New Year's party."

"You are not inviting my friend as your date. Get your own." Adam chugged the remainder of his beer and tossed the can.

Now they were getting somewhere. Something was definitely bugging him. "What's going on?"

"Nothing. I'm going to bed."

"Hey, man, you know I was just yanking your chain. I have enough of my own prospects. I don't need to poach." He immediately thought of Sydney and how pissed off she'd been.

"Yeah, I know."

"I'm here if you want to talk."

Adam shook his head and left the room. Hunter poured the rest of his beer down the sink, sacrilege to most guys he knew, but he'd only taken the beer because he thought Adam wanted to talk. Without Adam in the room to distract him, Hunter was left thinking about Sydney again.

The way she'd played in the practice room was awesome. He'd been hesitant to interrupt her, but once he heard the passion in her music, he'd known that she would be an excellent coach for him. He knew the basics and could muddle through, but once he became a teacher, he didn't want to just muddle through. He wanted to be able to teach any student whatever instrument he or she wanted to learn.

He had a natural ability for picking things up, but there were only so many hours in the day and so many classes he could take. Learning to play drums hadn't happened, but he knew that as a teacher, he'd encounter plenty of kids who would want to play.

Getting Sydney to teach him would accomplish a lot. He wanted to feed off her energy and love for the instrument. It wasn't enough for him to go through the motions. He could get that from watching a few videos. Plus, working with her would give him time to convince her to come to the New Year's Eve party as his date. By then, marching band would be over and he wouldn't have to worry about any repercussions. She'd be like any other girl he dated.

He scooped another handful of cereal into his mouth and crunched away, drowning out the voice in his head that clearly called him a liar.

CHAPTER THREE

"Come on, Syd, please?" Trish whined from behind the closed bedroom door. "It's not like you have plans."

"How would you know if I have plans?"

"Because you haven't had a date in so long, I can't even remember. Two years?"

Trish was right. It had been two years since she'd dated. Sydney had put it out of her mind for so long that it hadn't occurred to her to keep track of the time. Regardless, she had zero desire to double date with her sister and whatever boring guy she'd hooked.

Trish thumped against the door. "I'll owe you."

Syd rose and flung the door open. "Why do you need me? Go alone."

"Jenny was supposed to double date with us, but she's caught that horrendous flu going around. Dave's brother is in from out of town and Dave doesn't want to leave him alone. If I don't bring someone, he'll feel like a third wheel." She pressed her hands together like she was praying.

Syd rolled her eyes and crossed her arms. She

never liked any guy her sister dated, so she was sure this one would be a dud, too.

"It's one night. It's not like I expect you to fall for the guy. Just talk to him. Have dinner and a couple of drinks. That's it."

"Fine, but you owe me big."

"One more thing," Trish continued with a slight cringe.

This couldn't be good.

"We're going to a club downtown, so you have to dress up. And maybe—" she pointed at Syd's arms—"cover the tattoos. Tame your hair. This is a nice place, not a college frat party."

"If I have to make myself look like you, you owe me more than one."

Trish laughed. "Not like me. Just a bit less like you. A tiny bit. I don't know how this guy will feel about tats and spiky hair. It's not like I'm asking you to recolor your hair. A little concealment." She dashed out of the room, but Sydney didn't feel like following. Trish returned with one of her dresses. "Wear this."

Sydney looked at the sweater material. It stretched under her fingers. "Fine. It better be good food and you guys are popping for high-end alcohol." She winked at her sister. "It'll help keep me friendly."

An hour later, Sydney sat in the backseat of Dave's BMW, the leather cold on the backs of her thighs. Dave's brother, Ken, sat beside her, staring out the side window. Other than a quiet hello when they picked up Sydney and Trish, he hadn't spoken another word until they parked.

As they walked down the street behind Trish

and Dave, Ken leaned in and said, "I'm sorry about this. Blind dates usually suck. Don't feel the need to entertain me. I would've been fine if Dave left me at home."

His admission made Syd feel a bit more at ease. She shrugged. "Let's make the best of it. Dinner and drinks on them."

"Sounds good."

They walked into Andy's, a place Syd had never visited, but Trish and Dave had gone often enough that Sydney felt like she knew what to expect. The interior was dim and a band was already in full swing onstage. As they skirted past tables and toward the rear of the club, Ken placed his hand on the small of Syd's back. It was a polite gesture, but it did nothing for her.

She sat across from Trish, something Trish maneuvered so she could give Sydney meaningful looks in case Sydney said or did something wrong. Ken sat beside her, and her back was to the stage. They ordered drinks and Trish volunteered suggestions for their meals. Sydney let her do whatever she wanted because the waiter set a twenty-dollar glass of whiskey in front of her.

As she sipped, Sydney allowed the smooth jazz to wash over her, making it easy to tune out the conversation at the table. A swift kick to her shin jolted her attention. Trish stared with wide eyes.

Sydney bit her lip on a smile before saying, "Sorry. I got caught up in the music." She turned toward Ken. "I'm really into music. Although I'm a graphic design major, that's my backup plan. I play the drums. I hope to put together a band and start playing for money."

"No need to apologize. I could sit here and watch your face while you listen. It's fascinating."

Her cheeks warmed even though she didn't fully understand the compliment. She didn't think her face changed. Ken began telling her about his job—corporate attorney in Philadelphia. She tried to be interested, but the music kept tugging her attention.

After she finished her first drink, she excused herself to go to the bathroom and check out the band on the way. Just as she wound through the tables, the saxophone began a wailing solo, which reminded her of Hunter. She looked up and her heart thudded like a bass drum. Up on the stage Hunter stood front and center, backed by a group of middle-aged men.

Sydney froze and stared. His long hair had been smoothed and combed back neatly, but now fell forward. He looked like the music consumed him, but he loved it. She'd never seen him quite like this. Granted, she'd only seen him play on the field and then he mostly acted like it was a joke. This serious side of Hunter drew her in and made her want to plop down right there on the floor and absorb everything.

Jazz had never been her thing. She'd listened to it before. Any decent musician studied all kinds of music. This was the first time it made her feel something, even though she couldn't quite put her finger on it. Slow and languid, almost like he was begging for something. Her heart wrenched at the same time her blood raced. Pieces of the song echoed through her, but she couldn't name it.

As the song neared the end, he looked up and

straight into her eyes, but he couldn't have seen her because she stood in the shadows of other patrons and he had house lights on him. But she felt him searching. She pulled away, glancing at the ridiculous, so-not-her dress she wore, and scurried to the bathroom.

One thing she got out of this night was that Hunter Reed did not need her help with any kind of music.

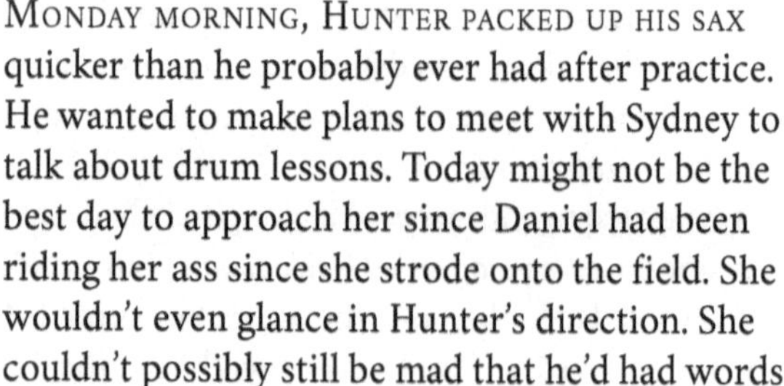

MONDAY MORNING, HUNTER PACKED UP HIS SAX quicker than he probably ever had after practice. He wanted to make plans to meet with Sydney to talk about drum lessons. Today might not be the best day to approach her since Daniel had been riding her ass since she strode onto the field. She wouldn't even glance in Hunter's direction. She couldn't possibly still be mad that he'd had words with Daniel last week.

Then again, he wanted to have a few more words with the asshole. But he didn't have time. He was supposed to meet with his adviser in less than ten minutes to talk about next quarter. He grabbed his case and looked for Sydney, but she was gone. He sighed and hoped she'd be in the practice room where he'd found her last week.

He ran to the education building and was only a little out of breath when he reached Dr. Hampton's office. She was waiting for him, as usual. He liked her because he knew she wanted him to succeed, but right now, she looked like he'd somehow managed to disappoint her.

"Hunter. How are you?" She stood behind her desk and gestured to the chair in front of her.

"I'm good." He sat, setting his sax case beside him.

"Looking forward to the holidays and break, I assume?" She returned to her seat and folded her hands primly on the desk.

Everything about Dr. Hampton was prim. Her puffy cloud of gray hair never appeared to move. Her thin lips were painted pale pink, never any other color. Her suits were tweed. Like, all of them. He wondered if she owned anything else. She embodied the image of stodgy old professor.

"Aren't we all looking forward to break?"

She nodded without actually agreeing with him. "I have some good news. We have you placed for student teaching."

"Excellent." All of his friends had gotten their assignments last week.

"You'll be at North Ridge High School. We were able to get both a history teacher and the band director to agree to work with you."

The way her head tilted, he knew there was some bad news, too. He braced himself.

"There were some concerns, however."

"Concerns?"

"When you completed your hours of observation at North Ridge, some of the teachers felt you were overly friendly with the students."

Her pause indicated that she expected some response. Too bad he didn't have one. "I thought part of the observation process was to observe and learn. I wasn't inappropriate with any students. It's not like I asked girls out on dates. I talked to students to get a feel for the school culture."

Dr. Hampton's palms separated and she moved her hands as she spoke. "That's all well and good, but the teachers felt you were not just learning, but trying to be friends with the students."

"I don't know what I did wrong."

"Hunter, you're a boisterous, friendly young man. People flock to you because of that. Your charisma serves you well. However, you need to learn to rein it in. If students see you as too laid-back, they'll take full advantage and your control will disappear. You have to find the balance between being friendly and being an authority figure."

Her words sank in and although he understood what she said, he had no idea how to accomplish it. He didn't want to be an authority figure. He wanted to help kids learn, help them enjoy history and music.

Dr. Hampton chuckled. Just what he needed, someone laughing at him.

"You look like you were just diagnosed with a life-threatening illness. You'll be fine, Mr. Reed. Take your break, come back refreshed and ready to be a teacher." She stood to let him know she was done.

He stood and said thank you as clearly as his tight throat would allow. He grabbed his sax and walked out. As the cold air blasted him, his mind cleared a little. He had over a month to figure it out.

He inhaled and the bitter sting of winter hit his lungs. The frigid air reminded him that he wanted to catch up with Sydney. He smiled at himself because he didn't really think she was cold, just reserved. Now more than ever he needed to have the best tools to be a teacher. He needed to prove to his adviser and other teachers that he would be good at this.

He jogged across the open quad to the arts building. The heated air warmed his numb cheeks. Hunter walked straight to the same room and hoped to find Sydney. Peering through the small rectangle of glass in the door, he was surprised to find her sitting at the drums, but not playing.

Shoving the door open, he didn't wait for her to acknowledge him. "Hi."

She looked up and wrinkled her forehead. "Hey. What are you doing here?"

"Looking for you. I tried to catch you after practice, but you have your vanishing act down. I figured you were ticked off at Daniel again, and I guessed this might be your go-to place to work off some steam."

"Yeah, well, I can't play and talk, so what do you want?" She twirled her drumsticks, gearing up for another song.

"I need your answer. Can you teach me?"

She swallowed hard and then let out a low chuckle. "No."

That was it. One word. No explanation. He'd expect that kind of response if he'd asked her to strip in the middle of the football field. "Why not?"

"You don't need my help. You don't need *any* help."

"What are you talking about? Why would I ask if I didn't need help?"

"Maybe what I should've said is stick with what you're good at."

In a few quick strides he was across the room. "I can't. What I'm good at isn't enough."

"Look, I saw you last night. At Andy's."

He jolted back. While he'd played he felt a niggling sensation of familiarity, but saw no one in the crowd. The thought of her being there made him uneasy. Playing at Andy's was personal and not something he shared. It rarely meshed with people's impression of him. Even though he was glad she hadn't, he still asked, "Why didn't you stop and say hi?"

"I was on a date."

Oh. Emma had told him she was single. Must be a new thing. "Okay. What does my playing at Andy's have to do with you not being willing to teach me?"

She stood and rounded the drums to stand in front of him. He caught the slight scent of her perfume, spicy and warm. The purple tips of her hair flicked in the light and gave her a weird halo effect. "I saw you play. You were amazing. You don't toss aside passion like that to fiddle around with a new instrument because you think it'll get you into my pants. You keep at it and hone it. And I'm *so* not the person to help you hone anything slow and jazzy."

Her eyes blazed while she spoke, like she was ready for battle. He reached up to shove his hand through his hair and forgot he was wearing his knit hat. Knocking it off and onto the floor, he growled in frustration. Sydney backed away as he bent to grab the hat. When he straightened, she'd moved far enough that he could no longer touch her, not that he would have. "I love playing at Andy's. The place is magical for me. But it's not enough. Andy's is not my life, my future."

Her arms shot up as she asked, "And you think playing drums is?"

He scrunched his hat in his hand and tried to explain. "No. Teaching is. I'm an education major. I want to teach kids. I'm a passable drummer, but I don't know enough to teach it. I don't know where I'll land next year, but I want to be ready for anything. Have you ever heard of a middle school or high school without a slew of kids wanting to be drummers? Drums are cool. Trumpets? Not really."

"You're going to teach?"

"Is it that hard to believe?"

"Well, you're...I don't know...a fun guy, like the class clown. I can't picture you all buttoned up and serious."

He pinched the bridge of his nose. What the fuck? He had no idea that being fun and being a good teacher had to be mutually exclusive. Two people within an hour telling him he couldn't be serious bugged the shit out of him. He could be serious when he needed to be. "Whatever."

He turned to grab his sax from where he'd set it.

"Wait. I wasn't trying to offend you."

Hunter stopped, but didn't turn.

"Is this paying gig at Andy's?"

Chuckling, he faced Sydney to see that she'd moved closer again. "No. You really think my band is a group of forty-plus-year-old guys? My regular band has a gig at The Garage on the weekends."

"Oh."

"Does that mean we have a deal?"

"I'm no teacher, but I can play. I don't know if I can give you what you're looking for. I know you won't ever play the drums like you played the sax last night. That's something that can't be taught."

"I don't need the feel-it-in-your-bones love for drums. I need to be able to help kids who feel that passion understand it and act on it."

He must've said the right words because Sydney smiled. A slow lift of her lips, almost like she didn't want to but couldn't help it. She shoved one stick into her back pocket and her hand darted out in front of her. "We'll give it a shot."

He took her hand, which was stronger than he'd thought, and shook. "Cool." Then he yanked her arm to pull her off balance and toward him. "Now you'll have to give me your phone number so we can keep in touch."

She braced a hand on his chest, dropping her other stick in the process. "Nice try, Tenor. This is a business arrangement. Nothing else."

He liked her hand on him and wanted to keep it there, but she righted herself and pulled back.

"Friendly business, though."

"Whatever." She picked up her stick.

Pulling out his phone, he added a new contact. "What's your number?"

She grabbed the phone and typed it in for him. He liked her take-charge, no-bullshit attitude.

"We practice tomorrow night. I'll text you my address."

"Do I have to bring anything?"

"Nope. I have all the instruments. Do you want our lesson to be before or after band practice?"

"Doesn't matter to me."

"After, then." That way, they would have time to get to know each other alone without interruption. "Assuming you won't be too worn-out after practice."

She shot him a cocky grin. "Don't worry about me. I can keep up. Can you?"

Without waiting for an answer, she returned to her drums and began beating out a rhythm. He took the hint and turned back to the door. As he swung it open, she stopped playing and called out, "Hey, Hunter."

He jerked back at the sound of her actually using his name. When his eyes met hers, she lost the cockiness and was dead serious. He thought maybe she had changed her mind.

"You can't tell anyone about this. Especially at band. It's just between us."

A strange request, but he had no issue with it. Band wouldn't be over until right before break, so even though he didn't think anything between them would cause trouble, he didn't want to take any chances. Her demand made him wonder about her reasons, though. "Sure."

He winked and slid out the door.

Sydney rolled down the street for a third time looking for a parking spot. Hunter hadn't said anything about his street being permit parking only. Her phone buzzed in the console. A text from Hunter: **Let me know when you get here. I have a permit for you to park.**

Figured. She pulled over in front of his apartment and answered. **I've circled three times trying to find a spot. Would've been good info to have. I'm in front.**

Be right there.

While she waited, she took in the quiet neighborhood. Not at all what she expected from a guy like Hunter. An old two-flat with flowerpots on the front porch. They were empty now, but she could imagine a riot of color spilling out in the summer. Many of the cars on the street were SUVs and minivans. The neighborhood screamed young families. What the hell was she doing here?

A blur ran past her windshield and it wasn't until he thunked against her window that she realized it was Hunter. She rolled the window down.

"Here." He shoved a piece of paper on her dashboard. "Park anywhere on the street. Want me to wait?"

"No. I got it."

"Good. It's freaking cold out here."

"Go figure. Late November in Chicago."

She rolled her window up as he ran by again. This time she noticed he didn't wear a jacket and it looked like he only had socks on his feet. Stupid guy.

She found a spot easily this time since it was still early in the evening. Mulling over the state of the neighborhood bought her some more time before going in. It wasn't just Hunter's home making her nervous. She was expected to work with his band, one that was established and had relationships and routines.

Neither of those things were her forte, which was a huge part of why the bands she'd started failed so quickly. She took a deep breath. If nothing else, this would be one hell of a learning experience. She'd find out how a successful band works, whether she had it in her to give drum lessons, and if she could fight the urge to crawl all over Hunter naked.

She grabbed her bag with the beginning drummer books she'd brought, shoved the door open, and let the cold air hit her. Hunter was all kinds of bad for her and she knew it. Unfortunately, she was always drawn most to what was bad for her.

Running up the sidewalk to the house, she was shocked to see the door swing open before she hit the porch. Hunter stood there waiting with a grin on his face that she knew attracted anything with two X chromosomes.

"What took you so long? I was beginning to think you changed your mind."

Rather than answering his question, she asked, "Where do we practice?"

"In here." He led the way into the first-floor apartment.

Inside the door, she paused. The entire living room was set up like a music practice room. What she wouldn't give to have this. He had an entire wall lined with instruments. One guy sat and strummed a guitar. The drum set was used, but in good shape. She looked behind Hunter and saw the dining room acted as their living room. She pointed to the instruments. "How does your roommate feel about the noise?"

"He knew I was like this when we moved in together. He doesn't care. He works a lot and does his own thing in his room."

She squinted to see more of the apartment, but everything past the dining room was dark.

"This is Jay. He's lead guitar. The other guys will be here soon."

Jay nodded at her and continued to strum. She waved at him.

"Okay." She set her bag on the floor near the door and dropped her coat on top of it. "You want me to hang out and get a feel for it today, or am I actually playing with you guys?" She rubbed her cold hands together.

"Uh, it's up to you. Kevin will be here, but he's cool with being done this weekend if you're ready to take over." He watched her hands twist. "You want a drink or a tour or anything?"

She shrugged. "A water would be good."

"Come on." He touched her arm and nodded toward the dark end of the apartment. He spread his arms out. "This is obviously the living room." As he got to the end of the room, he flipped a switch, bathing a small hallway in light. He pointed at a door on the left. "That's Adam's room."

He turned and brushed against her as he moved. She didn't know if it had been intentional, but the heat from his body felt good. He reached into the next room. "Bathroom." Then he turned again and pointed at another closed door. "My bedroom."

He winked, but didn't open the door or offer to show her around. He got some points for that.

"Kitchen's back here." Again he stepped around her, the barest of touches as he moved. It was a tight fit, but if he put in the effort, he could've moved without coming in contact with her. He said nothing more as he continued to walk away, so she followed. Before she even crossed the threshold of the kitchen, he had the light on and the refrigerator open. He pulled out a bottle of water.

She accepted it even though she wasn't thirsty. She'd wanted the tour, but didn't want him to know.

"We also have beer if you prefer."

"No. This is good."

She stood staring at him for a minute, just to take him in. This guy was a pile of contradictions.

Playboy on the field, serious jazz player, teacher wannabe; she wondered which one was really him.

"What? Do I have food on my face or something?"

She smiled. "No. I was just thinking."

"About?"

"Nothing important." Behind them, the noise in the living room increased, letting them know the rest of the band was there.

"I want to thank you for accepting my offer."

"Maybe you should hold that until after we have the first lesson. You might regret it yet."

He stepped closer. "Not likely."

And there it was again. The sizzling charge in the air between them that they both were aware of but didn't quite acknowledge. She gripped her water bottle tighter and swallowed. "We should probably get started. Your band is waiting for us."

He continued to stare intently into her eyes, but whispered, "Yeah."

For another second or two, neither of them moved, trapped by the buzz of attraction, until she blinked and stepped back. Hunter shook his head with a smile and led the way through the living room.

She was going to need a whole lot more strength to succeed with this arrangement. Hunter wasn't even trying and her brain was fuzzing out on her. She twisted the cap on her water and took a couple of gulps.

~

PRACTICE HAD NEVER FELT LIKE IT LASTED SO LONG

as it had tonight. They practiced their regular set plus a couple of other songs. Sydney sat in on the songs she knew and took notes when she didn't. Something about watching her scribble in a tiny notebook while her purple-tipped hair flounced around made him want to touch her, mess with her, grab her attention.

Because she wasn't giving him anything. Other than listening to basic directions, she focused solely on Kevin, which he supposed was good because she was taking over for Kevin, but Hunter half expected her to at least notice him. He wanted her to give him one of those looks she occasionally threw at him when they were on the football field, maybe a cocky wink because she sounded so damn good playing, but again, nothing.

While the other guys packed up their gear, Sydney continued to sit behind the drums. She looked like she was made to sit there. Jay and Kevin both glanced at her and at him like they were waiting for some confirmation that there was something else going on between them. Lance was oblivious, as usual. Hunter said nothing, knowing that if he did, Sydney would be pissed. Pissing her off on their first night together wouldn't be a smart move.

She shifted on the stool, like she wasn't sure what she should do while waiting for the guys to leave.

At the door, Jay looked at her. "See you Thursday?"

"Yep." She gave him one of her rare friendly smiles.

A little ping of jealousy hit Hunter. He wanted

one of those smiles for himself instead of the cocky, barely flirtatious ones he usually received. He enjoyed the flirty ones, but he'd never gotten the softer version. He briefly wondered what he'd have to do to earn one.

When the door clicked behind the guys, Hunter asked, "How do you want to start? Want another drink?"

She shook her head. "I'm good." Standing, she pointed at her bag near the door. "I brought a couple of my old beginner books for you to look at. I don't know how much you know."

He dragged a chair closer and sat. "I don't think I need to start like a six-year-old. I do understand music."

She puffed out her cheeks as she exhaled. "I told you I'm no teacher."

"What's the most important thing for me to know about drums?"

She closed her eyes and tipped her chin up a notch. "Rhythm. Nothing else matters." She dropped her sticks at her feet and began slapping her thighs.

Her eyes popped open and she nodded at him to follow her lead. He felt silly slapping his legs, like a little girl playing at camp. But then as soon as he thought he had the beat going, she changed the rhythm. It took him a second to adjust, but he did.

After a few minutes, she added a foot stomp in between beats. He continued, but it was pretty damn boring.

Finally, he asked, "What does slapping my hands and stomping my feet have to do with playing the drums? I know how to count off notes and find the beat."

Her palms smacked her legs one last time and stopped. "The drummer is the heart of the music. It's not just counting off notes. It's setting the tone for every piece." She straightened, and then added, "I get that you're used to playing with both hands. A lot of people have a hard time coordinating, so you start simple."

She slapped her right thigh. "Tom one." She slapped her left. "Tom two." She stomped her foot. "Bass."

"So you think when I'm teaching kids, I need to start with patty-cake?"

This time her sigh was pure irritation. "Kids who love the drums will feel the beat, they might instinctively understand rhythm, but you need to be able to explain it to them so they'll be able to read music. If they're some kind of savant, they'll play by ear and never need you, but most kids need some hand holding."

"Can we assume I am at least at the stage after hand holding? Since I have experience reading and playing music?"

"Of course. I thought you needed help teaching it, not just playing it."

Damn. She was right. He wouldn't be able to skip steps with most kids. "Wait. Sorry. You have a point. I thought if I understood how to play, I'd be able to teach it, but clapping like this never would've occurred to me."

She lifted a shoulder. "I'm sure other teachers would help you."

"How long do I keep up the slapping and stomping?"

"Until they understand the difference between eighth and quarter and sixteenth notes."

"That might take a while. Kids are impatient."

"So mix it up. Teach some rhythm. Let them hear and try to figure out the notes when a professional plays. Let them hold the sticks."

"The sticks?"

"Sticks are cool." She bent and grabbed hers, twirling one in place.

"That's the problem. Kids think they can sit down and start right there."

"Of course. So let 'em try and fail. Then they'll want you to teach them."

For the first time in years, nerves took over his body. He wouldn't be able to sell this. Kids would see right through him.

"Sometimes, you need to give them a taste, so they know what's coming."

"Huh?"

"Come here." She stood and backed away from the stool.

Hunter took her place and she handed him the extra sticks she'd left by the kit. He wrapped his fist around each stick.

Sydney leaned over his shoulder and reached for his hand. She peeled his fingers away and repositioned them. "Grip matters."

Her sexy whisper skittered across his neck and his dick perked up.

"Not too hard. You're not choking someone. And not flimsy. Nice and firm." Her fingers curled over his, warm, smooth, and firm.

He closed his eyes because he could totally imagine her whispering those words while they were naked. His pants were noticeably tighter. He shifted to find some relief and his shoulder connected with a tit. He expected her to pull away, but she didn't. She might've even leaned a little more into him.

"Find your rhythm," she said and then stepped away.

He stared at the two toms and struck the same beat they'd done against their legs.

"Whoa," she called.

He stopped and looked over his shoulder at her.

"If you pound away like that, you're going to do damage to your hands. Best case, some raging blisters. Worst case, tendonitis or carpal tunnel. Loosen your grip."

Again, her hands came over his and made the motions with him. He should've felt like an idiot, but he couldn't, not with her pressed against his back, her spicy perfume filling his senses. His mouth watered with the thought of tasting her skin.

She continued through a few measures before straightening. This time, he felt her arch her back. Her stomach grazed his arm as he continued to play. He wanted to make her move like that in bed and the picture in his head caused him to miss a beat.

Sydney shoved his shoulder. "That's enough for today. Don't you think? Practice basic rhythms, mix it up a little. If you want, we can read some music next time. I'm sure that'll be easy for you."

He stood, not wanting her to leave yet. "You want a beer now? Take a little break after all your hard work?"

She rolled her upper lip into her mouth and bit down. She might've been trying to hide a smile. At least he hoped so.

"It's a beer. I promise I won't tell anyone."

"A beer would be good."

And that was the window of opportunity he was looking for. Hunter now knew he'd break down whatever barrier had kept her icy for months. She was at least a little interested in him. He'd worked with less.

hat the hell was she doing? More important, how did Hunter get her to do this? She was supposed to play with the band, give a quick lesson, and leave. Having a beer alone with him wasn't part of the plan. Then again, neither was touching him or laughing with him and she'd done both in abundance tonight.

It had been easier when the rest of the band had been present, though. Once they left and the drum lesson started, she relaxed a little too much, let her guard slip. And being up close and personal with Hunter stirred things in her she didn't want stirred.

She followed him back to the kitchen. Sharing a drink there would help keep things cool.

As he reached into the refrigerator, he asked, "So what are your plans after graduation?"

"I don't graduate until next year."

He spun with two bottles of beer. "Are you old enough to drink this or am I going to get in trouble for contributing to the delinquency of a minor?"

She snatched the bottle. "I'm old enough. Wanna card me?" She twisted the cap off and took a swig. "I took some time off so I'm a year behind." Sitting in one of the two chairs at the table, she decided that was enough of an explanation.

"Is that why you don't want anyone from band to know about our arrangement?"

She nodded. "You're leaving. A few more practices and a game and you're done. I have to come back for another year."

"I won't be here, so what's the problem?"

"I'm going to offend you if I say it."

"I don't offend easily."

"You have a reputation for being a man whore. I don't want anyone looking at me like I'm one of your playthings." The partial truth dried her throat, so she drank quickly.

For a moment, he said nothing, just watched her with his warm, friendly eyes. He really wasn't offended.

"Fair enough." He dragged the other chair closer to her, close enough that his knees almost bumped hers. "Between you and me, I date a lot. I don't think there's anything wrong with that. But I'm far from a man whore."

She wanted to believe him. She didn't, but she wanted to, which was a whole level of disturbing she didn't want to pick apart. "How long have you and the band been together?"

He sat back in the chair, stretching his legs out in front of him, so one passed between hers and settled beneath her chair. "Me, Jay, and Lance have been together since high school. Our drummer took off to California. I met Kevin freshman year."

"Wow. You guys have been working together since high school?"

"We didn't actually work back then. We wanted to impress girls. We didn't start paying jobs until college."

She turned her bottle in slow circles. "Why not play professionally?"

"We do. We'll probably continue after graduation, but this is a hobby for us. I want a steady job with a real paycheck. If I had to rely on music to take care of me, I'd probably grow to resent it. Playing wouldn't be fun anymore. I don't like to do things that aren't fun."

"Huh." She hadn't thought about it that way. She couldn't imagine not loving music.

Hunter leaned forward, bringing his legs back and bracing his elbows on his knees. "What are your plans?"

Her mouth dried once again with his proximity. She'd do much better if he kept his laid-back, I-don't-need-anything distance. When he leaned close like this, she felt like nothing else in the world could capture his attention. It was part of his charm and she couldn't afford to get drawn in.

"After you do graduate?" he prompted.

Great. Now she looked like an idiot who couldn't hold a conversation. "I hope to put together my own band and play full-time."

He angled his head slightly, but didn't move back. "Why college, then? You don't need a degree to play."

"I promised my parents I would finish. My major is graphic design, so I can do freelance work while I build a reputation for playing." The explanation tightened her nerves. She should be able to tell him. Of all the people she knew, Hunter would understand her need to play.

"What is it?" he asked quietly.

"I'm good at graphic design. I could make a living at it, but I'm afraid it'll suck the life out of me. I want to play music."

"So play. If it's right for you, go for it."

She smiled and huffed a little laugh. "Sounds great, except I haven't been able to put together a band much less get hired. Three times I've tried and failed. I feel like I'm spinning my wheels, going nowhere, and I'm already so far behind everyone else." More than a year wasted with a guy who didn't really care, a year of schooling tossed aside. The embarrassment over her choices still stung.

"Behind how?"

"Look at you." She waved with her free hand. "You have an established band that plays for money and you don't even want to do that for a living. You're on track to graduate on time and have your career set." She took a quick drink, unused to being this honest with anyone. "I've got nothing but some random ideas."

"Who says you have to have your whole life figured out right now?" He laid his hand on her thigh, sending a shock wave of warmth straight north. "You'll be fine."

She nodded, afraid to say anything because she just might blurt out, "Kiss me." And she didn't want that.

Definitely not.

Clearing her throat, she set her bottle on the table. "I should get going."

He stood slowly and she watched the length of his body straighten. He only took a half step back, so when she stood, they were nearly touching.

"It was a good practice. I'm glad you were here."

"Me too," she said, but she wasn't entirely sure what she was agreeing to. She blinked to regain her thought process and tried to step away, but only succeeded in crashing into the chair she'd vacated. Grabbing the back of the seat to steady it, she shook her head. She'd promised herself she wouldn't let a guy like him have this effect on her.

As she straightened, another question popped into her head. "What song was it? That night at Andy's."

"I played a lot of songs that night."

She shot him a look. "You know which one. You did an amazing solo."

His head lifted with recognition. "'Have a Little Faith in Me.'"

He said it more like a request instead of a song title and the urge to bolt hit her again. She pointed over her shoulder and left the room without looking back.

He followed. When she reached for her jacket, he beat her to it and held it out for her to slide into. Once her arms were in, he bundled the front together and zipped it up for her.

"It's cold out. Wouldn't want you getting sick."

His fingers were warm on her neck as he straightened her collar. She didn't know who moved first, but suddenly their bodies collided and he hauled her up for a wet kiss. His hands grabbed her head and moved her where he wanted her. Drowning in his strength, she fought for oxygen, stealing it from his lungs.

The kiss made her dizzy and hot and sexy. And so freaking turned on. Hunter pushed her against the wall, the hard length of him pinning her upper body. She gripped his hair and wanted to climb him. Raising her leg to wrap around his, she thrust her hips into him, loving the way she made him hard. His heart pounded as out of control as hers.

It wasn't until he pulled away to come up for air that she came to her senses. She pulled her leg back and wanted to melt away. Hunter braced hands on the wall beside her head. He lowered his face, staring into her eyes as he panted. He wanted more. She saw it plainly. So did she, but that was the kind of move she'd sworn off.

Pressing a hand to his chest over his still-throbbing heart, she pushed and slid away. "That shouldn't have happened."

"It was pretty fucking fun."

She clenched her jaw to stop the smile. Any indication that she had enjoyed it as much as he did would be an open invitation. She shook her head.

A feather-light touch brushed her neck below her earlobe and down the side. "You can try to hide your reaction, but you're not that good an actress. My friend Free can give you lessons if you want. In the meantime, you're not fooling me."

Heat rushed across her skin. She knew she couldn't hide anything. That was why she liked to keep her distance. She licked her lips and tasted his kiss. "I don't want this. I just got done telling you ten minutes ago that I won't be one of your playthings."

"And I thought I was clear that I don't treat women like playthings. I date women. I've dated a lot of women. Nothing stuck." He threaded his fingers into her hair, tugging until she looked at him. "I'm not playing games. I want you. Let's see where this goes."

Crap. This was more bizarre than she'd considered. She figured him for wanting a quick roll. Exploring with him put her far out of her element. "Not a good idea."

"Your kiss tells me otherwise." He yanked her zipper up higher. "You want me to go warm up your car for you?"

Huh? The offer jolted her. No pressure to stay and continue what they'd started. No urging to commit to something. Just a gentlemanly offer to warm her car. "No, thanks. I'll be fine."

He stepped away and opened the front door for her. She shuffled to leave, confused by everything.

"Hey," he called as she stepped into the hall.

When she turned, he held out her bag. She reached for it, his fingers grazing hers, sending yet another surge of desire through her. Oh, man, did she have it bad. "Thanks."

"See you tomorrow at practice."

"Not if I see you first." She tried for a grin, but had a feeling that she looked more crazy than funny.

He waited in the chilly hall until she was out the front door. She resisted the urge to look back once she got outside. She needed to get away from

him to gather her senses. Maybe she should suggest they only do lessons in the practice rooms at
school. Surely that would prevent anything from
happening between them. Coming to his apartment and being alone with him wasn't smart.

She wouldn't lie to herself and say she wasn't
attracted to him. She just needed to control it. By
the time she got home, it was late, but Trish was
waiting up.

"Where have you been?"

"I told you I was practicing with a new band.
I'm going to be filling in for their drummer for a
few weeks. Then I gave a drum lesson."

"Hmm-mm. What's his name?"

"Who?"

"The guy who kept you out late on a school
night."

"I'm fine, *Mom*." She knew Trish would be irritated by the comment. She prided herself on being
the cool big sister.

"I'm not scolding you."

"Using a word like *scold* totally ruins your cred-
ibility as cool. You know that, right?"

"Whatever. I'm glad you're finally venturing
out. Is he cute?"

"Very." Crap. She hadn't wanted to say it out
loud.

"Ha! I knew it." Trish patted the couch beside
her. "I want details."

"No details. His name is Hunter. I know him
from marching band. He needs drum lessons and a
drummer for his band. I fit the bill."

"Maybe that's how it started, but you have that
look. The one that says much more happened."

Sydney let her bag slide to the floor with a sigh. "He kissed me before I left. But it was nothing. I told him I wasn't looking for anything like that." She added a nod as if it would make it all more convincing.

"Why would you do that? You need to go out, Syd. Have fun. Just don't let it get out of hand."

Like last time. The words went unspoken, but they hung in the air. The problem was, she didn't know if she could have fun without it getting out of hand. Especially with a guy like Hunter. "I am having fun. This is a great opportunity for me to play in a real band, making money. And if I'm successful with the drum lessons, I have one more way to earn cash."

"There's more to life than making money."

"I know that, but I need to support myself."

"You need to have fun."

"Playing is fun. This is what I want and I'm not about to put it aside for a guy." Not again. Never again. "I want to finish school so I have something to fall back on. If I've learned anything from the last few years, it's to have a backup plan."

Trish stood and tossed a pillow on the couch. "You know I admire your determination, but this is the time when you're supposed to explore and screw up. Enjoy yourself before going out into the real world." She patted Syd's shoulder as she walked by. "I'm going to bed."

"Me, too. Practice is early." As she moved toward her room, Sydney thought about her sister's words. She'd already done plenty of screwing up and she hated how it made her feel. But she missed having fun. Being with Hunter tonight had been fun. Playing with the band, the lesson, the beer and the conversation, but most of all the out-of-control kiss. She sighed again. She'd give anything for an easy answer to this dilemma.

Listen to her head or her body? Only one had a habit of letting her down.

CHAPTER SIX

The following morning, Hunter sat on the field, freezing his ass off, waiting for Sydney to show. As usual, she jogged from the parking lot at the last minute. She never came early, didn't stop to chat with people, just walked with her head down.

At least until she neared him. The look she shot him was both heated and pleading. He could almost hear the words *Please don't tell anyone we kissed.* He licked his lips and smiled. She ducked her head again. Instead of saying anything, he played part of "Have a Little Faith in Me," hoping she'd recognize it.

Of course she didn't acknowledge him, but the set of her shoulders relaxed a bit. They only ran through the drill for an hour since it was so cold. Saturday would be the last game of the season. His last game as a member of the marching band. He'd miss it, but he was ready to move on.

As soon as they were released, he made his way to Sydney. He wanted to let her know what songs they'd practice tomorrow so she could prepare. "Hey, got a minute?"

She paused and turned to face him. Her cheeks were bright pink and she narrowed her eyes. "What?"

She had the act down pretty good, as long as he didn't actually look into her eyes. There, he saw amusement, not annoyance.

Before Hunter could say anything else, Daniel stood between them. "Oh, crap, Peters. Really? I thought you were better than to fall for his line of shit."

Her face went from pink to red. Her mouth dropped open. "I didn't—"

Daniel cut her off. "I guess that makes you a Reed sucker, huh?" He smacked the arm of the drummer to his left. "Get it? His name is Reed."

Hunter caught a glimpse of tears in Sydney's eyes before he turned on Daniel. Dropping his sax, he shoved Daniel with both arms. Caught off guard, Daniel stumbled back.

"What the fuck, Reed?"

"Where the fuck do you get off talking to a girl like that?"

"Defending your girlfriend now?"

Hunter didn't think about how it would look or what the consequences might be. His fist shot out and caught Daniel's jaw. His head snapped back. The sound of Daniel's teeth clanking to-gether and the throb in his own hand offered a lot of satisfaction.

Hunter braced for a fight. The musicians around them huddled close, not wanting to miss anything. Two guys from the drum line grabbed Daniel and held his arms.

"It's not worth it, man. Our last game is Saturday. You don't want to get tossed out for fighting."

The words hit home for Hunter. He could end up missing his last game.

Daniel sneered at him. "Learn to take a joke, asshole."

Hunter ground his teeth together so he wouldn't respond. Daniel's friends led him away. A nudge at his arm pulled his attention. Mike stood there to hand him his sax.

"He's had that coming for a long time. I'm surprised you didn't get a round of applause for it."

"Thanks." He turned in a circle to find Sydney, but she was gone. No surprise, really. He took his sax from Mike and inspected it for damage. As the crowd dispersed, he scanned for Sydney's purple hair.

Emma came up beside him, pulling on thick gloves. "She left. She was really upset."

"I figured." He wanted to ask if Emma thought she'd answer her phone, but then he remembered he'd promised not to say anything to anyone, especially at band. "Check on her, okay?"

"I will." She started to walk away, but then turned. "It's good that you stood up for her. But I hope it wasn't part of your usual procedure. She deserves better."

"I have no idea what that was." The simple truth struck him. He liked Sydney, but starting a fight over a girl had never been his style. Then he remembered the look of shock and hurt in her eyes at Daniel's words. He'd do it all over again even if it meant he got tossed off band.

He packed his saxophone and looked across the field. He wanted to go after Sydney, but he didn't know where she was. She wouldn't likely go to the practice rooms. He zipped up his jacket and went to the parking lot. He'd text her. That would give her space if she wanted, but also allow him to apologize.

He got to his minivan and pulled up short. Sydney was leaning against the sliding door, her bag at her feet while she rubbed her bare hands together.

"Hey," he said.

Her eyes shot up. "'Bout time."

She'd been waiting for him. His heart thumped a little, knowing she couldn't be too mad at him. He got closer and realized she was probably numb from standing in the cold. "Crap. Hold on." He pressed the fob to unlock the doors. "Get in and warm up."

Instead of walking around to the passenger door, she slid open the side door and climbed into the backseat. He climbed in after her, tossing his saxophone case over the seat and into the back. He closed the door and reached over the driver's seat and started the engine.

"We'll have heat in a minute." He tugged off his gloves and offered them to her, but she shook her head. He dropped the gloves and held her hands between his. They were like ice. "How'd you know this was my car?"

She smiled. "How many guys drive minivans?

Everyone makes fun of this thing. Don't you know that?"

"It hauls all the equipment every week, and it gets me where I need to go." He kept rubbing her hands even after the blower starting sending warmth their way.

She tried to pull away, but he held her.

"I'm sorry about what happened. I wanted to give you the playlist for tomorrow night's practice so you could at least familiarize yourself with the songs. And I wanted to give you this." He pulled a parking permit from his pocket. "I didn't think it would cause all that."

"I know. Daniel's an asshole. He probably doesn't even really think anything is going on between us. He likes to make me miserable by giving me a hard time."

"Is there something going on between us?" he asked quietly.

She bit the corner of her lip. "I wish there wasn't, but there's something. That kiss last night…"

"Was pretty fucking hot."

She laughed then, loud, and her entire face opened up like he'd never seen. Totally unguarded. He definitely wanted more.

"It was, but I wasn't joking. I can't deal with more of what Daniel dished out."

He scooted closer to her, reading between the lines. "So you're open to exploring what we have as long as no one finds out."

She pressed her lips together and didn't answer. Hunter laid his hand on her thigh, which was still cold through her jeans. He leaned toward her ear. "I'm great at secrets. We only have one more practice and a game. I can guarantee no one will know."

Her breath hitched as his nose brushed the shell of her ear. From the corner of his eye, he saw her lick her lips. Just the tip of her pink tongue darted out. His mimicked the motion against the spot below her earlobe. There, her skin was warm.

"Stop."

The strangled word made him freeze. He eased back and looked into her eyes. There he saw a hint of fear mixed with the lust. What had made her so afraid?

She swallowed hard. "I can't explore with you right now."

But she was willing. His dick got hard thinking about it. "Soon?"

She nodded. "Until then, it's like you don't even know me."

"Won't people get suspicious if I don't at least try to flirt with you? I've been doing it for months."

A slow smile crept back. "I can't stop you if you play a song, but don't expect a reaction from me."

"We'll see."

She slid away from him and yanked the handle on the opposite door. A blast of cold air swept in, but she turned back to him. She moved in quickly and kissed his cheek. "Thanks for standing up to Daniel."

It was on the tip of his tongue to ask if no one had ever stood up for her, but he knew she wouldn't answer. So he went back to comfortable ground. "How soon are we talking?"

"Very." Then she slipped out the door and slammed it behind her.

Sydney definitely knew how to get to him. He shifted and waited for the hard-on to go away.

He turned off the car and ran to class, barely making it on time, but he couldn't stop thinking about Sydney and the idea of having her soon.

As soon as class let out, he texted her. **Free for dinner?**

Her response was quick. **I'm not dating you.**

Can't blame a guy for trying.

I have class tonight. Won't get home till 10. You can stop by for a drink.

Damn. The girl wasn't kidding when she'd said soon. **Send me the address and I'll be there.**

He didn't have another class until the afternoon, so he went to meet Free for lunch. It had still been dark out when Free had called him to ask to meet, which meant only one thing: girl trouble. Knowing Free, he didn't get any sleep and when he discovered he couldn't solve his problem on his own, he called Hunter.

Of the three of them, Free had always been the shyest. He'd been geeky, even more than Adam, which said something. The whole acting thing helped him come out of his shell, but it never extended past the stage unless he wore a costume. Hunter had no idea how he planned to work for his dad where he'd need to deal with clients.

Hunter drove to the sub shop in their childhood neighborhood. Hot lunch might've been a better choice, but a sub in the middle of the day was guy food. It was where they'd gone every time they cut class or snuck out when they were grounded.

Free's car was already in the lot, engine still running. Hunter parked and tapped on Free's window as he walked by. He didn't wait for his friend because it was too damn cold. Inside, he unzipped his leather jacket and waited. Free came in a minute later, with a goofy hat on his head, pom-pom and all.

Hunter pointed at it. "Didn't we outgrow that stuff about fifteen years ago?"

Free shrugged. "It's warm."

"So what's wrong?"

"Who said anything was wrong?"

"You called me at five thirty this morning to make lunch plans. What's her name?"

Tugging off his hat, Free blew out a hard breath, puffing his cheeks like a trumpet player. "Let's order first."

"I knew it."

They placed their orders for foot-long Italian subs, extra dressing. They grabbed a booth and as they unrolled their sandwiches, Hunter said, "Shoot."

Without looking up from his food, Free said, "There's this girl, Samantha."

"Knew it," Hunter said around a mouthful of bread and meat.

"I met her at the coffee shop near the gym where I meet Cary."

"Have you talked to her yet?" With most guys, if they said they'd met a girl, he wouldn't have to ask, but with Free, *meeting* could just as easily mean he'd seen her and made eye contact.

"Yeah. A couple of times." He bit into his sandwich.

Hunter waited, shoving more food into his mouth.

"I even bought her a cup of coffee."

"Wait a minute. You said you met her after the gym?"

Free nodded.

"So you were wearing one of your crazy costumes."

"That's just it. Every time I've seen her, I've been coming from the gym. She's only seen me in costume."

"Hmm…I don't know if it's a positive or a negative. She's seen you at your craziest: plus. If she's not weirded out by it: minus." Hunter knew Free's motivation behind wearing the costumes was to help his brother while he worked out to lose weight, but to strangers, Free just looked strange.

Free shrugged. "I think she likes it. Even before I talked to her, I saw her watching me, like waiting to see how I'd be dressed. The last couple of times, she asked to take my picture."

"Are you sure she's not a crazy?"

"She seems normal. She's studying to be a social worker, so she's in the area every day for volunteer work at some shelter."

"What's the problem?"

"She's only seen me in costume at the coffee shop. How do I move past that?"

"That's your problem? Easy—ask her out."

"Easy for you, maybe." Free picked at the lettuce on his sandwich.

Hunter set down his half-eaten sub and wiped his hands on a napkin. "Are you seeing her today?"

"Hopefully."

"So today, when you sit down to drink your coffee, tell her that although you like your brief meetings, you'd like to extend your time with her. Ask her if she's free for dinner." He felt sorry for Free. He couldn't imagine being afraid of women. Hunter had been a natural flirt his whole life. Free had always been unsure of himself.

"Just like that? Tell her I want to go out with her?"

"Yeah. Did you think there was some magic to it? I just ask. She has no way of knowing how you feel unless you tell her. Maybe she's thinking you're a strange guy who likes to chat over coffee. I've seen you flirt. You can't throw out a line to save your life. You need the direct approach." He picked up his sandwich again. "The worst that happens is that she says no."

"Then what?"

Hunter thought of Sydney. "If you really want her, you try again. Some women appreciate persistence."

"And some would call you a stalker."

Hunter laughed. "Hopefully, you get the hint before that point."

As they finished their meal, they talked about plans for the New Year's Eve party, Hunter effectively shutting down Free's annual idea of having a costume party. The guy needed to get comfortable in his own skin. His dad wouldn't let him play dress-up at work. Getting used to life without costumes would be Free's resolution.

Hunter thought again about Sydney. What kind of resolution would she have? Then he decided she wouldn't have one. She was the kind of girl who wanted to live without regrets.

CHAPTER SEVEN

Sydney unlocked the apartment door and found only the kitchen light on, which meant Trish was already in bed. She would never know Syd had invited Hunter over.

Syd raced through the living room and her bedroom, straightening up. She had no idea what had gotten into her. She knew going out with Hunter was a mistake. Everyone in band would know. But this wasn't dating. This was sex. And if she didn't get some soon, she might explode. Ever since their kiss, she couldn't stop thinking about him.

Watching him punch Daniel had made her hotter.

She had just enough time to change her clothes and freshen up before Hunter texted to say he was almost there. She told him not to ring the bell because Trish was sleeping, so she went down to wait for him.

Standing in her bare feet wasn't the wisest choice because when she opened the door to let Hunter in, she also allowed a gust of cold air to follow. Instead of greeting him, she said, "Damn. It's cold. Follow me." She ran up the stairs to the apartment and heard his heavy steps behind her.

When they were both in the apartment with the door closed, she looked him over. She liked his worn leather jacket. It gave him the appearance of a bad boy. "Hi."

"How was class?" he asked quietly.

She invited the guy over for sex and he asked about class. She had no idea what to think of him. Pressing against him, she went up on tiptoe and kissed his cold lips. His hands immediately came to her face, stroking her cheeks and then threading into her hair. She loved the strong yet gentle way he held her.

Pulling away for a breath, she asked, "Did you want a drink?"

"Whatever you want."

She grabbed his hand and pulled him toward her bedroom. Closing the door and clicking the lock, she said, "We have to be quiet. Trish has to work early."

He took off his jacket and tossed it on her chair. "You sure about this?"

"As long as it remains just between us, I'm totally sure."

He dipped his head and tasted her lips, but it wasn't enough for her. Being alone with him, feeling the hard press of his body, all she could think about was getting him naked. She tugged at his T-shirt to feel the smooth skin beneath.

He reached over his head and yanked the shirt off one-handed. That made one hell of a GIF for her to replay in her mind later. She kissed his chest and down his stomach. The bulge in his pants let her know he was more than ready to go. She unbuttoned his jeans and slid them down his hips. His dick strained against his boxer briefs. She stroked him through the cotton before peeling the waistband down and kissing the head.

He groaned and stiffened. She lowered to her knees and took him in her mouth. He tangled his fingers in her hair again and guided her head. She hummed with the applied pressure and he grunted. He throbbed in her mouth and she got aroused knowing she knocked him as off balance as he did her.

Hissing, he pulled away. "Come here." He hauled her to her feet and pulled her clothes off. One minute she was dressed, the next, she wore nothing. He closed in again, but instead of feasting on her mouth, he went for her neck. He licked and kissed and sucked until she was panting. His fingers moved to her boobs and tugged on her nipples.

Gripping her hips, he pulled her forward, maneuvering her toward the bed. He shook his hips a couple of times to make his pants and underwear drop to his ankles and then stepped out of them. He kissed her again, and his dick prodded her stomach. His hands were all over, like he was a damn octopus, as if he needed to touch every inch of her. Except the one place she craved his touch.

"God, please touch me, already."

"I'm touching everything."

"You know what I mean, Hunter."

A wicked grin crossed his face. "Like this?" he whispered in her ear. His hand moved south and his middle finger slid across her slit. "Already wet." He groaned again, the vibration of his voice weakening her knees.

He banded an arm around her waist and kissed her like his life depended on it while his fingers stroked her until she trembled.

"Please tell me you have a condom."

"In my jeans, but we don't need it yet."

"Yeah, we do. I want you inside me."

"I want you to come like this, right now." His fingers thrust into her and his thumb circled her clit.

With him moving like that, it wouldn't take long. He felt so damn good. She clasped his shoulders for balance, her nails digging into his flesh. Her forehead thumped against his chest. Her orgasm spiked and Hunter kissed her to stifle her moan.

He shifted and bent to pick up his jeans, but he kept one hand on her hip as if he thought she couldn't stand on her own. He was right.

Letting go of her, he sat on the edge of the bed and rolled the condom on. "Come here."

He pulled her close, nudging her legs wide with his knees. He wanted her to straddle him.

She laughed. "I don't think my legs have the strength for that workout."

"I got you covered."

She climbed onto his lap and he guided himself into her. She sighed as her eyes rolled back. Over the last two years she'd tried to convince herself she wasn't missing much, but God had she missed this.

With his hands on her ass cheeks, Hunter lifted

her and brought her back down. When they connected, his pelvic bone bumped her clit, sending a shock through her. He eased back and created a calming rhythm.

As her legs regained their strength, she began to move with him, but he never gave her full control. He moved her shoulders back so he could suck on her nipples again and she tightened on his dick.

"I'm almost there. You?"

"I'm good."

"You'll be better." He licked his thumb and rubbed her clit again as his mouth latched onto her nipple.

The assault to her senses overwhelmed her. The octopus was back and he was all over her. The orgasm built again and she forced herself up and close to him. She wanted to be pressed against his body to feel his slick skin when she came. His hands moved back to her hips, his own pistoning quickly. She bit his shoulder as she came. Moments later, Hunter's body stiffened and he pulsed inside her.

They sat like that for a long time, with her sitting on his lap, head on his shoulder, his arms wrapped tightly around her. Their hearts raced in time, and their erratic breathing was the only sound in the room.

~

FINGERS ON HER BACK WOKE HER. SYDNEY squinted against the sunlight and looked over her shoulder. Hunter traced her tattoo. A sharp rap on the door made her jump.

"Hey, girl, you're late for class. Get your ass in gear. I'll see you tonight."

Sydney rolled over and slapped a hand on Hunter's mouth. She waited until she heard the front door close. Panic stole through her. "Fuck. What time is it?"

Hunter rolled away and checked his phone. "Eight thirty."

"Damn it."

"What?"

"I have a nine o'clock class. That I'm obviously going to miss. Fuck."

"Shit. I'm sorry. You didn't say anything last night and I didn't think about setting an alarm. We were both pretty spent." He sat up and swung his legs off the bed. "If we hurry, maybe you'll make it for part of the class."

She climbed out of bed with tears clawing at her throat. How had she let this happen? The first time she slept with a guy since Tony and she was already fucking up. Gathering clothes from her dresser, she did everything she could to avoid making eye contact with Hunter. She knew it wasn't his fault she'd missed class, but she wanted to blame him.

"Hey," he said from behind her. The heat from his body warmed her back. His arms circled her and he kissed her head. "You go take a shower and I'll make you some coffee. You'll get there. No big deal."

He had no idea how big a deal it was. This was

how it had started last time. A missed class here or there. No big deal. Until it was.

"Thanks," she mumbled and left the room.

By the time she got out of the shower and dressed, Hunter had a to-go cup of coffee ready for her. He was fully clothed, even wearing his jacket.

"I left it black."

She dumped in a heaping mound of sugar. "Sorry to make you rush like this."

"No problem. I don't have class until ten." He pulled his keys out. "I'll see you tonight, right?"

"Yeah."

"Don't forget the parking permit I gave you yesterday."

He pressed a quick kiss to her lips and walked out the door. Sydney stomped down the stairs and ran to her car. She hadn't missed a class all semester, so this shouldn't be an issue, but finals were coming up. It'd be just her luck that she'd miss something vital today.

She needed to learn to not get caught up in a guy, stay on track. But Trish had been right. She missed having fun, and sleeping with Hunter had been fabulous.

She continued her self-talk all the way to school. Hunter hadn't been anything like Tony. There had been no manipulation to get her to sleep in and cuddle with him. Hunter had apologized for making her late and even made her a coffee. As much as she appreciated it, though, it was more than she expected or even wanted from a guy she was sleeping with.

THAT EVENING, SYDNEY GOT A SPOT RIGHT IN front of Hunter's apartment, glad she already had the permit in her window. Nerves skittered through her. Her life suddenly felt very unsettled and that was all due to Hunter. She'd accepted that she wouldn't have any relationships until after she graduated. She was okay with it. He was making a mess of everything, but not necessarily in a bad way. She hoped.

Grabbing her bag, she ran up to the house. The sound hit her through the door. Hunter was playing. That man knew how to play a ballad. If it wasn't so freaking cold out, she would've stood on the porch and just listened. But the cold seeped through her layers, so she rang the bell.

Less than a minute later, Hunter answered the door with his sax in hand. He wore a T-shirt and sweatpants. His hair hung loose and brushed his jaw. He swiped it back as she stepped through the door. Her eyes were drawn to his arm and the defined muscle that bulged there. "Hey."

"Aren't you freezing?" she asked.

"Nah. The apartment's warm." He turned and walked back into the front room.

She closed the door behind her and followed. As she unwrapped her scarf and pulled off her jacket, she said, "You can finish. It sounded good from outside."

"I was just messing around, warming up."

She glanced at him. He looked like maybe he was embarrassed about her hearing. It didn't fit her image of him. "I'd like to hear the rest."

"You'll hear plenty as soon as the others show. How was school?"

The switch of topic surprised her. They didn't talk about school. They discussed music and marching band, their common interests. "Okay, I guess. I have some killer finals coming up next week."

"Me too. But then we have a month off to relax."

"Do you have gigs planned for the whole break? I mean, for the band."

"Yeah. We usually play a few extra nights since we have no class. I have to check with the bar. I'll let you know when I have a schedule." He watched her carefully as she took the spot behind the drums.

"Is there a problem? Kevin's not coming tonight, right?"

"No. We're, uh, having a New Year's Eve party here. You want to come?"

A party at Hunter's house. A party was public, far from keeping their exploration a secret. "I don't think so."

"Band will be over."

"But I still have to deal with band members after you graduate."

He waved a hand. "They'll forget all about me by next summer."

Again, he had a point. New Year's was still more than two weeks away. They might be done by then. "We'll see."

The bell rang and Hunter went to let the guys in. Lance and Jay were together when Hunter came back. Sydney didn't know if they traveled together or just had great timing. They both smiled and said hi when they saw her.

"'Bad Reputation' must've been your contribution," Jay said as he took off his coat.

She blushed at the mention. When Hunter had given her the playlist for this weekend, "Bad Reputation" was a new addition. "Not my idea, but Hunter heard me playing it."

"I like it. Good choice."

Lance nodded in agreement. For the singer of the group, he didn't seem to talk much. Their friendliness surprised her. She was only a temp, someone with no weight in the group, no real say, and she'd be gone in a few weeks.

Although she wished Hunter hadn't added a song for her, she appreciated it. Hunter didn't say anything as they warmed up and got ready to play. In fact, he barely took notice of her. If only he could remember to do that at marching band practice, her life would be so much easier.

"Let's start with 'Bad Reputation' since it's new," Hunter said when they were all ready.

All eyes turned to her. The attention overwhelmed her for a second. Hunter winked and the nerves eased. She counted off in her head and began to play. The song was easily one of her favorites, both because the beat was so strong and because the lyrics suited her. And Hunter, she suddenly realized. Lance began to sing, but he tripped up at the first verse because of the word *girl*.

"I can't sing *girl*. I can say I'm a lot of things, but that ain't one."

Sydney snickered. "So substitute *guy*."

He smiled at her, his lips lifted at a crooked angle. "Maybe you should sing."

"Sorry. No one wants to hear that. I sound bad even in the shower."

Jay leaned over to see her around Lance's shoulder. "Maybe we need a demonstration."

Hunter smacked him in the head, making Sydney laugh again. "Stop acting like you've never been around a chick." He pointed at Syd. "From the top."

This time they made it through without a hitch. Then they played again, sounding even better. She'd forgotten how much fun it could be to play with other musicians. Marching band didn't count.

After "Bad Reputation," they moved on to the rest of the set, which were all male-dominated fuck-the-world kind of songs. They were all so different from the music she heard Hunter play when he was alone or at Andy's. She wondered if Lance and Jay knew about his other gig.

Throughout the set, Hunter bounced between instruments. He played the sax, the keyboard, and even the guitar. He excelled at everything he touched. It made her remember his hands on her. Pushing the thought aside, she focused on the music. She didn't want to miss a beat.

She had a great time playing, and when they were done hours later, sweat trickled down her back and between her boobs. She'd have to remember to dress in easily removable layers for Friday night. As Jay packed up his guitar, he looked back and forth between Hunter and Sydney, like he wanted to ask something. Hunter seemed oblivious to it.

She met his gaze and raised her eyebrows in question. He turned to Hunter and said, "Hey, man, could you grab me a bottle of water to go?"

"Sure." Hunter left the room and Jay came close.

"Is there a problem?" she asked.

"Nope. I like you. I like the way you play. But I see the way he looks at you. Is that going to be a problem?"

How Hunter looked at her? She couldn't even figure out what that meant. "How does he look at me?"

"A cross between wanting to rip off your clothes and raise you on a pedestal."

"I agree with the first half. We have chemistry. You're way off on the second, but there's nothing to worry about. We're having fun. That's it."

"Make sure he's on the same page. He's my friend and I don't want him to get screwed over."

Sydney's skin prickled with awareness, so Hunter must've come back into the room. Jay stepped away, so she didn't answer him, not that she had a clue what to say. Like she would ever have the power to screw Hunter over.

Hunter tossed the water bottle at Jay. "What's going on?"

"Nothing," Jay answered. "See you tomorrow night."

Syd watched them leave and tried to process what felt like a warning from Jay. Hunter reached out, handing her a bottle of water, too. She took it, drank a few gulps, and then asked, "Ready for your lesson?"

"In a minute. What happened with Jay?"

"Nothing."

"You looked spooked. Did he say something to upset you?"

The flash of anger in his eyes made her realize he was gearing up to defend her again. "No. Actually, I think he's trying to protect you. He asked what was going on between us. I told him we're having fun and there was nothing to worry about."

"And?"

"He told me to make sure you're on the same page. Why's that? Do I strike him as the kind of person who lies or something?"

"Not you."

She'd stepped in it now. Hunter ran a hand through his hair, smoothing it back. She said nothing, unsure how to proceed. Luckily for her, Hunter continued.

"I told you I've known Jay since we were teenagers."

Syd nodded.

"In high school, I had this girlfriend, Shelly. We were in marching band and concert band, so we spent a lot of time together and had all the same friends. I thought we were serious." He sat beside Sydney behind the drums. Their thighs touched, sending more warmth through her body.

"Let me guess: She didn't think it was serious."

He nodded. "She broke up with me and took our friends with her."

Sydney laid a hand on his leg. "That's shitty. But it was also high school. We all have crappy high school stories." And some, like her, had mistakes that extended into college.

"Yeah. I'm over it."

He sounded sure of himself. Almost believable.

"Wait a minute." She nudged his knee with hers. "So I just got a if-you-hurt-my-friend-I'm-gonna-hurt-you talk from Jay?"

"I guess so."

"I don't know if I should feel honored or threatened."

"Honored. Totally." He wrapped an arm around her neck and pulled her close for a quick kiss.

She yanked back. "We're not supposed to be doing this."

CHAPTER EIGHT

"You agreed to explore." When she was this close, he had a hard time remembering any of her objections. He took an exaggerated look around the apartment. "Part of the deal was that no one from band could know. There's no one here."

She sighed, knowing she had no argument. He moved in for another kiss. This time, she didn't pull away. With his hand at her nape, her hair brushing the back of his hand, he guided her to him.

She kissed like she played drums: all in.

It had only taken a few minutes with their lips locked, tongues tangling, for her to surge forward. She climbed onto his lap, notching herself against him.

His dick fought against his zipper for release. Hunter kissed along her jaw and down her neck. Her pulse thumped against his lips, and he tasted her sweat. She rocked her hips and he groaned. God, he wanted her naked.

Sydney yanked a fistful of his hair to grab his

attention. He looked up at her and moved toward her mouth again. She leaned back, keeping him at arm's length.

"We need to stop," she panted.

She was so hot against him. Keeping a grip on her hips, he shifted so she could feel how hard she'd made him. *By kissing.* A small whimper escaped her mouth before she pressed her lips closed.

"I swear I can keep a secret." His words were more like a growl.

"It's not that. Although after what happened with Daniel, I have my doubts. I have to focus on school."

"Is this about missing class?"

"Yeah. I can't afford that."

Again, he knew there was more she wasn't saying.

Pressing on his shoulders, she climbed off his lap. She turned and bent over to grab the bottle of water she'd set on the floor.

Her ass poked right in front of him, so he squeezed. Maybe groped a little. She squealed and spun around.

He raised his hands in surrender. "It was right there. I couldn't help myself. How about dinner on Saturday? Band and regular classes will be over then. Just finals after that."

She squinted one eye. "Okay. Until then, nothing." She uncapped the water bottle and took a swig. "Ready for your lesson?"

Crap. He'd already had one lesson on self-restraint. "No. Not unless I'm pulling my dick out to use as a drumstick."

She giggled. He tried to give her a dirty look, but when he saw the sweet smile on her face, he couldn't.

"Sorry. Things got a little out of hand again. I tried to stop you." A little shake of her head said she wasn't the least bit sorry for his condition.

He closed his eyes and thought about unsexy things. Tuba players. Free dressed like the Riddler. Band uniforms. Old Mrs. Thompson who lived across the street and had eight cats. He inhaled deeply. All he had to do was keep his distance for two days.

When he reopened his eyes, her head was tilted back and her throat worked as she chugged the remaining water in the bottle. He thought again of Mrs. Thompson—in a bikini. Mission accomplished.

"Okay. Today's lesson."

Sydney smirked. "Are you still going to be okay if I come back behind the drums?"

"I'll try."

When she strode over, she took her stool and moved it over a few inches so they would no longer be touching. He hoped it would be enough to help with his focus. She pulled out sheet music and set it on the tom in front of him. With her stick, she pointed to notes, explaining as she went.

After a half hour, Hunter realized he wasn't absorbing anything other than the scent of her warm skin. He laid a hand over hers. "Can we just play a song? I'm not getting this."

"You're not getting this because you keep thinking about getting into my pants."

"Guilty. So let's play and get my mind off it. Teach me 'Bad Reputation.'"

"You're not ready for that."

"Try me."

She gave him a little shove away from the drums and started to play. When she paused, he pointed with his own stick for her to scoot away. He might suck at reading the music she put in front of him, but he had a great ear and picked it up fast. He repeated her actions. While not as fast or as smooth as she'd played, it was acceptable. Acceptable wasn't good enough for him, though, so he did it again.

When he looked over, Sydney was shoving her sticks into her bag.

"Where are you going?"

"Like I said before, you don't need lessons. You certainly don't need my bumbling attempts to teach you."

He jumped from the stool and dropped his sticks. "I learn fast, but because I've never had lessons, the basic stuff you're giving me is great. I'm never going to play drums for me. I need those little things, like tapping out a rhythm on my lap. I don't know that stuff."

Everything he said was true, but mostly, he didn't want her to cut out. He liked hanging out with her.

"How about a beer?"

"Not tonight. I have studying to do. Finals next week. If I'm playing with you tomorrow night, at the game on Saturday, and then going out Saturday night, I need time to study."

"Okay. Water to go?"

She nodded. "Thanks." Then she went back to shoving things into her bag.

When he came back from the kitchen, she took the water. "Do the guys know you play at Andy's?"

"Yeah, why?"

"It seemed like it was a secret or something. The music you play there, the music I heard when I came in today, it's not like what you play with the band."

"I like variety."

"You should play like that more often. It's who you are. I saw it at Andy's and I heard it from the porch. Those songs, the ballads, are…God, they're full of so much emotion."

"Like you playing 'Bad Reputation'?"

She nodded again. "They mean something to you."

He lifted a shoulder. He didn't often like to talk about what music did to him. "I play music at The Garage because I get paid to do something I like. We play what people want to hear. When I'm at Andy's it's a different crowd, so I play different music."

"But you prefer one of those slow ballads to everything else, don't you?" Her warm brown eyes stared at him knowingly.

"Yeah. I like the slow emotion of them. The way you don't have to hear the words to feel what the song is expressing."

She slid her arms into her jacket and then stepped close. "I think I need help with my zipper again. It's cold out there," she whispered.

"You trying to test me or kill me?" he said as he tugged to close the jacket.

"Maybe I just wanted a good-bye kiss."

The zipper hissed between them as he slid it up. He didn't need to pull her close because she rose up to brush her lips against his. He angled his head to take the kiss deeper. If he wasn't going to be able to touch her for two more days, he needed to make this one count.

His fingers found the soft skin of her neck and he stroked it as he thrust his tongue past her lips. Their breath mingled and their tongues tangled. Her hands moved across his chest, around his back and lower until she had a palm full of ass cheek. She groped him the way he had her and in doing so brought her hips crashing into his. He was hard again but thinking it away wasn't possible.

Hunter eased back and straightened the collar of her jacket. "Go study. See you tomorrow."

"I like the way you talk about music almost as much as I like to hear you play it."

Whoa. Hearing her talk like that was almost as good as the whimper she made on his lap. "Any requests for tomorrow? It's our last practice together."

"Surprise me." She grabbed her bag and left.

He looked out the front window as she got into her car and waited for it to warm up. Jay had wondered if Hunter was on the same page as Sydney. Having fun. As she pulled away, Hunter questioned if that was all they had. It felt like a lot more.

$$\backsim$$

Friday night, Sydney paced through the small living room. Nerves tightened every muscle in her body. She'd thought getting through her last marching band practice with Hunter would be hard. For the most part, he acted as though he'd never laid eyes on her, which was exactly what she'd asked for, but it stung. She didn't think he'd be so good at it.

But then as they were dismissed, he broke out in song. He'd played the same song as when she'd arrived at his house yesterday. She'd stopped in her tracks, and although she didn't turn to look at him, she listened. She closed her eyes and felt the music, the way he'd described. The song was painful but beautiful.

She'd always seen Hunter as the party guy, quick with a joke, a laugh, a smile. Yet when she heard him play like that, it was nothing short of heartbreak.

Now, standing in her apartment, all she felt was fear. She was supposed to play her first paying gig tonight and all she could think was that she would screw it up.

Hunter texted to ask if she wanted to drive together. The Garage was closer to her house than his, so he offered to pick her up. It was probably for the best because she wouldn't be able to back out.

She rolled her shoulders. She could handle this. This was what she wanted to do with the rest of her life, so she needed to get over the nerves.

But that was where the fear took hold. If she screwed this up, she'd be stuck with her backup plan and she really didn't want that.

Trisha came home then and tossed her keys on the counter. "What time do you guys go on?"

"Uh, eight, I think."

Trish glanced into the kitchen at the clock on the microwave. "You should get going then, don't you think?"

"Uh-huh. Hunter's on his way to get me."

"This is the kisser?"

Syd rolled her eyes, but nodded. Trisha didn't know about him spending the night, and she wanted to keep it that way. She shook out her arms and inhaled deeply. She definitely couldn't think about kissing Hunter. Or anything with Hunter, for that matter.

Throwing her arms around Syd's shoulders, Trish squeezed and said, "Don't be nervous. You got this. I'll be there to cheer you on."

"No."

"You can't stop me. I want to see my baby sister rock."

"Oh God. Please don't talk like that in the bar."

"I promise not to embarrass you."

The bell rang and Syd grabbed her jacket and an extra set of sticks, just in case. "See you later."

"Break a leg."

She ran down the stairs and walked out to meet Hunter.

"I don't get invited in?" he asked.

"We have to go, don't we?"

"I would've made time for you to give me an official tour of your apartment."

"I'll introduce you to my sister later. She said she's coming to the show, so she can give me a ride home if you want." She tugged her gloves on and followed him to his van. "Did you have to load everything up yourself?"

"It's not too bad. I had my roommate help."

She felt bad, though, because the drums took up a lot of space and had to involve multiple trips. "I could've come to help. I'm using your drums."

He started the car. "No big deal. And I'll drive you home."

Without thinking about why, she decided she liked that. Her nerves settled somewhat, but she tried not to attribute it to Hunter's presence.

They drove in silence for a while, except for the radio playing some smooth jazz. She found it almost funny that he geared up for a rock concert by putting on easy listening. But then she remembered how he explained his love of the music.

"I liked what you played on the field today."

"I cheated. I didn't learn something new. It was the song you heard me playing at home."

"I know, but I really listened this time. It's a sad song, right?"

"I guess. It was 'Let Her Go' by Passenger." He started to hum and then picked up with some lyrics. As soon as she heard the words, she recognized the song. It was a lonely, painful kind of song, about loss and missing what you once had.

He stopped without finishing the song. Syd looked at him. "Life isn't fair."

"What do you mean?"

"Not only can you play just about any instrument you pick up, but you can sing, too. It's not normal, and certainly not fair." Plus he was gorgeous with great hair and an even better smile, which she absolutely refused to say out loud.

Of course, he chose then to turn his killer smile on her. "Don't hate me. I can't help that I was born gifted."

"You have to be bad at something. I'd feel a whole lot better if I knew what." She was only partially joking.

"I suck at being organized, which means I'm late a lot."

He'd never been late for marching band, so she wasn't sure she believed him. She waited for more.

He shot her a look out of the corner of his eye. "I suck at math. That's why I chose history as my second major. I can't draw. My roommate, Adam, is an artist, so if I ever need a drawing, I go to him. I'd just embarrass myself."

"I'm still not feeling the balance here."

He drove down an alley and pulled up behind a brick building. Pointing at a green metal door, he said, "This is the back entrance. Jay and Lance are here to help unload. Sit tight." He took out his phone and sent a text, then got out and opened the hatch.

Syd sat stunned for a minute. Sit tight? She got out of the car and went to the back to carry in the instruments. "If I'm part of the band, even temporarily, I should help. I can handle carrying in the drums."

Lance and Jay came through the door. Lance held it open as she walked through carrying the bass. With the four of them moving, it only took a few trips. Jay brought his own guitar and Hunter brought the keyboard, his guitar, and the drums. He also had the amps and microphones. She wondered how he'd managed to accrue so much equipment. She made a mental note to ask him about it later.

They were the first band on for the night. As they set up onstage, Sydney's nerves returned tenfold. What she'd imagined as a small dive bar actually had a huge audience waiting for them. They set up the instruments and went to the bar to have a quick drink.

Lance downed a shot of whiskey. Jay and Hunter each had a beer. Sydney opted for water. She feared alcohol might not stay down.

Hunter ran a hand down her arm and leaned close. "You okay?"

"Nervous. I didn't think the crowd would be so big."

"You'll be fine." His hand slid down and he interlocked fingers with hers. "We'll start with 'Bad Reputation.' You could probably play it in your sleep."

She nodded and hoped he was right. They finished their drinks and went backstage to wait for their introduction. Hunter still held her hand and she let him even though it mostly broke every rule she'd set for them. She was too anxious to care.

Backstage, he pulled her down the hall, into a dimly lit space.

"Take a deep breath."

She did.

"Look at me." When she didn't immediately respond, he cupped her jaw and tilted her face up. "Nothing to be nervous about. Just like playing in my living room."

When she looked into his eyes, it seemed simple.

He stepped closer and kissed her. A gentle lip lock and quick swipe of his tongue. She tasted the beer he'd drunk, but was quickly swept up in the feel of him. Her stomach settled even though her heart continued to race.

Hunter pulled back. "Better?"

She smiled. "Just one more thing you're really good at."

THE SMILE ON SYDNEY'S FACE MADE HUNTER'S lungs freeze. It was better than the smile she gave other people because she was open and un-guarded. With a sudden fierceness, he realized he wanted more of this. He wanted to capture this feeling, this moment.

"Would you prefer I tried to suck at kissing?"

She laughed and it echoed off the bare walls in the hall. "God no. I was making a point."

"That's a relief. I like kissing you. You're pretty damn good at it yourself." He pulled her hand and they moved back down the hall. "You ready?"

"I have to be." She straightened her spine and lifted her chin.

He loved the way she could change herself like that. In a heartbeat, she could bury her vulnera-bility so no one saw. That she didn't hide it from him made Hunter feel even better. He'd finally gotten past some of her defenses and all it took was some kissing that he'd completely enjoyed.

They played their set, including an encore. Sydney was great. She blended in with the guys, and by the end of the night, they were all laughing and joking as they loaded his van. Once all the equipment was stowed, they went back to the bar for a drink.

"Can I buy you a beer?" he asked Sydney.

"No, thanks."

"Crap. That's right. You have studying to do. We can get out of here."

"No. It's okay. It's not too late. Have your drink. I can find my sister and get a ride with her." She pulled her phone out as she spoke.

He took her phone. "I want to spend time with you. If all I get is a ride to your apartment, that's what I'll take. I drink with these guys all the time."

Her face filled with suspicion.

"No games. Let's go." He waved to Lance and Jay, who nodded and smiled at Sydney. "Do you want to find your sister and let her know you're going home?"

"If I had my phone, I'd text her."

He handed her phone back. "Sorry."

She sent a text and a minute later she looked up. "Trish is already gone. She said she stayed for most of our set but had a headache so she went home."

"See? You need me." He put an arm around her shoulder and waited for her usual slide away, but she allowed the casual touch.

He led her out the back door and into the alley where his van sat. He unlocked the door and opened it for her. "You were good tonight. Was it what you expected?"

She sat and waited for him to get in. "It was different. I've never played for a real audience. You know, people who came for the music, not family members who feel obligated, like at school concerts."

"Did you like it?"

"Are you kidding? It was a total rush, everything a little kid dreams of when she thinks about rock stars. I can't imagine playing in a stadium. This was a pretty small venue, but amazing."

"That rush is hard to find in other places. People who don't perform don't get it."

"You really want to give that up to teach a bunch of snotty kids?"

"I enjoy the rush, but it's fleeting. There's no stability. Working with kids is a different kind of rush."

He drove through the city on what he hoped would be the busiest streets to prolong the trip. They talked about the bar and Jay and Lance. The trip was shorter than he wanted.

When he pulled up in front of her apartment, she said, "I know I said I'd introduce you to Trish, but since she has a headache, she's probably in bed. Tomorrow night?"

"Sure. Get some studying done so you won't be distracted when you're with me."

She leaned across the console and gave him a quick kiss. "I can't imagine anything that would occupy my mind when I'm alone with you."

And just like that his dick was hard again.

She pulled the handle to open the door. "Hey, how were you able to afford all the instruments and equipment? That's a lot of stuff you're hauling around."

As soon as she asked, her eyes widened. "Sorry. That was nosy. You don't have to answer."

He smiled at her nervousness. "It's no big deal. My parents divorced when I was in high school. I took ample advantage of their guilt." He pointed over his shoulder. "What you see back there is a lot of parental guilt."

She laughed and slapped a hand over her mouth. Through her fingers, she said, "You're terrible."

"It's not like they didn't know I was taking advantage. They didn't care."

She shook her head almost like she didn't believe him and slid out the door. "See you tomorrow," she called as she closed the door. At the entrance to the building, she turned and waved at him.

Tomorrow couldn't come fast enough.

CHAPTER NINE

Saturday was a whirlwind of a party. The football game was one of the best of the season, which was a great way to end the last home game of the year. They played a post-game victory set for the players. The entire afternoon, Hunter did everything he could to avoid looking at Sydney. On field or off, he made a point of talking with other tenors. They invited him out for pizza and beer after the game, but the only thing on his mind was a date alone with Sydney.

As soon as he got into his van, he texted her to ask what time he could pick her up.

Give me a chance to get off the field. Jeez.

He could hear her snickery comment as if she sat next to him. He checked the time. Allowing for the hellacious drive home and a shower and then the drive to her apartment, he texted back, **I'll be there at seven.**

I'll be waiting.

He liked the idea of her waiting for him. He wondered if she was as excited as he was. He hadn't felt this way about a date in years. He had a tendency to keep things casual, and while what he had going with Sydney wasn't necessarily serious, it had the potential to be. He felt it. Keeping their attraction a secret added a layer of hot lust he'd never experienced.

At home, he showered and changed. Adam was out again, and he wondered what was going on with him and Reese. For a guy who swore he wasn't into her, he sure spent a lot of time with the girl.

Sydney hadn't mentioned where she wanted to go for dinner, but since she seemed like she preferred to keep it casual, that's how he dressed. At seven, he rang her bell and she buzzed him up.

At the second floor, she waited in the door to her apartment and he lost the ability to think. She wore a black barely-there skirt that rode so high on her thighs he wanted to crawl on his knees and beg for the chance to look up it. Her top was a purplish blue that shimmered and accented the colored tips of her hair.

"Are you just going to stand there all night and stare or are you coming in?"

How the hell could she be so calm?

"You look gorgeous."

Her cheeks flushed and, without thinking, he reached out to stroke one to feel the warmth.

"I promised you a tour and an introduction to my sister." Her voice was suddenly husky and he realized she wasn't as unaffected as she'd acted. She grabbed his hand and pulled him through the door, kicking it closed with her bare foot.

She pointed at a tall blonde. "This is my sister, Trish."

He shook Trish's hand. Even if Sydney hadn't been there to introduce them, he would've known they were related. They had the same warm brown eyes. "Hope you're feeling better."

"I am." Her smile was quick and genuine. "Sorry I didn't get to meet you yesterday. What I heard was great."

"No big deal. Glad to meet you now."

"Trish is heading out to dinner with her boyfriend." Sydney tugged on her sister's sleeve.

"Nice to meet you." She waved at Hunter and then pointed at Sydney. "Don't stay out too late. You still have finals to study for."

"Yes, Mom," Sydney replied in a snotty voice.

Trish rolled her eyes and put on her jacket. The scene was obviously one they'd played out many times.

As soon as the door closed behind Trish, he pulled Sydney close. "Band is officially over." She smiled up at him, which he took as an invitation. He pressed her close and lowered to kiss her.

What he thought would be a brief hello kiss quickly morphed into blood-pounding lust. Sydney's hips wiggled in his hands and bumped into him, making him hard again. He thrust a thigh between her legs, making her skirt slide dangerously high.

Heat from her pussy permeated his jeans so he pressed harder. She moaned into his mouth and fisted one hand in his hair. She held tight, just shy of being painful.

He tore his mouth away from hers, but didn't remove his leg. "We're supposed to be doing a tour and then going to dinner."

She narrowed her eyes. Then she pointed over her left shoulder. "Kitchen. We're standing in the living room. And if you follow me, I'll give you a detailed tour of my bedroom."

His dick twitched. His brain was losing blood too fast. "What about dinner?"

"Not hungry. For food at least." She stepped back and crooked a finger at him.

He didn't need to be told twice. He followed her to her bedroom. She flicked on the light, but completely lied about a detailed tour. As soon as they crossed the threshold, she slammed the door and pinned him against it with her entire body.

She began unbuttoning his shirt. Licking her way down his chest with each inch of exposed skin. He tried to grab her shirt, but she moved too fast for him to get a grip. She slid his shirt off his shoulders, but the cuffs stuck on his wrists. She grunted in frustration. "Tell you what," he said. "I'll get this off. You get rid of yours."

As he unbuttoned the cuffs, she whipped her top off, leaving her standing in a black bra and her skirt, which was no longer keeping her decent. Hunter stepped away from the door and slid his hands up her thighs. He stroked her through a scrap of silk, and her breath shuddered. Her panties were damp, but he wanted her all wet. He shoved the skirt up and peeled away the panties, dropping to his knees to get them off her feet.

Her trim pussy was at face level. He elbowed her thighs wider and buried his face between her legs. He kept one hand braced on her hip and the other reached around for a handful of her gorgeous ass, which pressed his shoulder into her thigh, lifting it, giving him better access.

She leaned back and gripped the footboard of the bed for balance, but didn't move away from him. Her other hand dove deep into his hair, all the way to the scalp and held him to her.

"Oh, fuck," she moaned.

He knew he'd hit the right spot, so he flicked his tongue faster. She was so fucking wet, he just wanted more. He moved his hand from her ass, and thrust two fingers into her. Curling and stroking those fingers while his tongue worked her clit. She began bouncing on his face.

"Don't stop. Don't stop," she kept repeating. As if he'd even consider it.

Her body stiffened and her hand on his hair tightened. Her thighs trembled and he lapped at her, loving the taste of her come. She started to slide away and he knew it was totally worth losing a handful of hair if he got to do that again. He crawled up her body and pushed her onto the bed, scooting her back from the footboard.

Her arms flopped out at her sides. She breathed heavily and looked at him below hooded lids. "I think you ruined me."

"I'm nowhere near done ruining you."

"I'd return the favor, but I don't think I can move yet."

"You just stay right where you are." He covered her body with his and slid a hand beneath her to release her bra. He pulled it away and took a moment to look at her tits. They were on the small side, but fit his palm nicely. He squeezed and licked and when he pinched her nipples, she responded with a low moan and a roll of her hips.

Fuck, he loved the way she responded to everything. How had he ever thought she could be icy? When she thrust her hips up to his, she ground painfully into his hard cock. He needed to get rid of his jeans and push inside her.

Her fingers were already fumbling with the button as he rose up to free himself. Hunter got off the bed and finished stripping. By the time be climbed back, she had a condom waiting. He reached for the rubber, but she pulled it away.

"Let me touch first." Her cool fingers wrapped around him and stroked.

His entire body went rigid. "Syd." He forced her name out, hoping she'd understand.

But she liked to play, so instead of giving him the condom, or even putting it on him herself, she ran her tongue down the length of him. She hummed on the return trip.

He gripped her shoulders and forced her away. "Not now."

She giggled and handed him the condom. Leaning back on her elbows, she watched him slide it on and licked her lips as he did.

She'd pay for that.

He covered her and settled between her legs. As he guided himself into her, she wrapped her calves around his hips. He sank deep and groaned with the pleasure. She met his every thrust. Everything about her was fantastic.

She pulled him close for a kiss and their tongues tangled as their bodies collided. He picked up the pace and she growled, "Deeper." He lifted her leg and drove in, burying himself to the hilt. Her muscles gripped him and he knew she was close again.

So he slowed and didn't thrust as deep or as hard.

Her eyes flew open.

He rocked gently.

"What are you doing?"

"Enjoying myself." Yeah, he was reveling this payback.

With both hands, she grabbed his ass and pulled him into her. "Stop playing games, Reed."

He lowered his mouth to her ear. "Like you played with me?"

"Okay, I'm sorry." Her hips wiggled against him. "Just finish."

He splayed her thighs wide and went deep again. He found a sweet spot he wanted to live and die in, but he couldn't hold out anymore. Driving into her until every muscle went rigid and she screamed, Hunter pressed his face into the soft curve of her neck. As her body milked him, he emptied into her and collapsed.

Her soft limbs slid away, boneless, but he didn't lift his head. He loved the smell and taste of her. After catching his breath, he rolled off her and removed the condom. Sydney didn't even move.

"Uh, where's the bathroom?" His voice was rough and craggy.

She raised her arm and waved in the general direction of the door. "Hall. Left."

He disposed of the condom and returned to the bedroom. Sydney hadn't left the spot where she lay. "Are you okay?"

"Uh-huh."

He stared at her a minute and tried to decide what his next move should be. Her naked body was one hell of a distraction, though.

"Could you maybe not stare?"

"Sorry." But he wasn't. Not even a little bit. He nudged her leg. "Hey, let's get some dinner."

She swung her legs off the bed. Standing, she smoothed her skirt back into place and then bent to retrieve her top. He grabbed his jeans and did his best to not think about the fact that she no longer had panties on under the skirt.

"Where do you want to go?"

She turned and watched him dress. "We don't have to go anywhere. I'm sure I can make some sandwiches or something. Maybe a frozen pizza."

As boring as the food sounded, being alone with her made the decision easy. "Sure."

He shoved his arms into the sleeves of his shirt and thought he heard her sigh when he pulled the front together to button it.

"Meet me in the kitchen." She left the room and he finished dressing, leaving his shoes off.

When he found her, Sydney had the oven on, a pizza on top of the stove, and peanut butter and grape jelly sitting on the counter. He was suddenly starving.

As she unwrapped the pizza, he stepped to the counter and pulled bread from the bag for sandwiches. "PB and J for you?"

"Sure. Light on the jelly, though. The pizza shouldn't take too long."

"So you live with your sister. Where's the rest of your family?"

"My parents live in a small town in central Illinois."

"Why aren't you going home for Christmas?"

"I am. Just for a couple of days, though. For me, this is home. I love being in the city."

She slid the pizza into the oven and he handed her a sandwich. She took a bite and studied him.

"Did I actually screw up making a sandwich?"

She shook her head. "It's good. What about your family?"

"My mom lives in Naperville with her new husband, and my dad lives on the far northwest side."

"So you have multiple Christmases to attend."

Not that he looked forward to any of them. Except for going to Adam's mom's house. "I speed through the holidays as fast as I can. Even after all these years, there's an undertone of animosity my parents have for each other. I like going to Bonnie's house. Adam's mom. She makes a huge meal even though it's just her and Adam. And me."

SYDNEY SWALLOWED THE LUMP OF BREAD AND peanut butter. Something about standing in her kitchen, sharing a cheap meal with Hunter and talking about family was more intimate than having sex with him. It made her uncomfortable. He seemed totally at ease telling her anything. He never backed off any question she tossed out.

He finished his sandwich before she'd eaten half of hers.

"Another?" she asked.

"Yeah. I worked up an appetite."

"I'm going to see about a movie." She left him to make his sandwich. She needed to get some space. She had no idea what had come over her. She'd finally agreed to a date with him because band was over and then she couldn't resist jumping his bones as soon as he walked through the door.

Guys like him were her Kryptonite. She knew it. She'd avoided them for the last couple of years. Why she thought she could handle this escaped her. The sex had been great—no, better than great. And it had been so long since she'd had great sex. Maybe the hormones were messing her up.

Hunter came into the living room carrying his sandwich like he didn't have a care in the world. He looked at the TV. "Thought you were looking for a movie."

She quickly grabbed the remote and clicked the TV on. Sitting in the corner of the couch, she focused on flipping through the channels, but she felt him staring at her. Finally, she handed him the remote. "What?"

"Nothing." He plopped next to her, close enough to touch, but not actually touching.

"What finals do you have to study for?"

"I have a handle on most of my classes, but biology is killing me."

"Biology?"

"I needed a science and I've avoided taking it until now. It's so freaking boring. Every time I look at my notes, I realize I fell asleep in class. The professor doesn't help. He speaks in a monotone like he isn't even interested in what he's teaching."

She'd shifted her body to face Hunter as she spoke. She didn't know how he did it, but he made her talk freely. It was rare for her to offer so many details.

"I can't help with science. If it was history, I'd be your guide."

She believed he'd make one hell of a guide for just about anything. Some stupid commercial for car insurance blabbered behind her. "Are you going to pick a movie or something?"

He shoved the last bit of bread into his mouth. His gaze traveled along her bare legs. "I might be able to pay attention to the TV if you changed. Wearing that, knowing you didn't put on underwear, the TV can't compete."

Her skin warmed everywhere his eyes wandered. She pushed up and straddled his lap.

"Fuck. What are you trying to do to me?" he growled as his hands came around to hold her ass.

"Having fun. That's what you wanted, right?"

"Hmm-mmm. I want it all."

His words gave her pause. All what? But since she wasn't sure she wanted the answer, she leaned down and kissed him. He hardened beneath her and she wanted more. She wanted him touching her again, stroking her, pushing into her. She didn't want to be lured into deep conversations that were more real to her than they were to him.

She didn't want him to pretend, and guys didn't pretend at sex. That was always real. She ground her hips against him. He reached under her shirt and pinched a nipple. The pleasure-pain of it shot through her. Pressing her forehead against his shoulder, she lifted up to undo his jeans.

"Condom. Pocket." He lifted his entire body and pulled a condom out. Then he shoved the top of his jeans low.

She rubbed herself on his hard dick, her body twitching when he bumped her clit. She was already close to coming. As soon as the condom was on, she rose up.

"Wait, let me—"

She didn't know what he planned to say because his words faded as she lowered herself onto him. He stretched her and filled her, but she still wanted more. She began to bounce on him and he pulled her shirt up and sucked on her nipples.

Gripping his hair, she moved faster, the tension coiling and tightening low in her belly. Yanking his hair to force his head back, she kissed him again. This time when her body came down her pelvis rubbed against his at just the right angle to press her clit.

Her breath came in short gasps. With his hands on her hips, he held her in place and moved in some magical way that had her seeing stars. What little oxygen she'd had dissipated.

"Good?" he ground out.

She barely nodded. He thrust up into her, lifting his hips off the couch and turned them so she lay on her back. He pounded into her like a jackrabbit, but she held on, her arms and legs wrapped around him until he shuddered and came.

The oven beeped to let them know the pizza was ready. They both opened their eyes and laughed. He eased out of her and pulled off the condom. "I'll take care of the pizza. You go change into some regular clothes or you won't be eating or studying."

He had no idea how little the threat meant to her. She mentally slapped herself. She was doing it again. Great sex was just that. It was not a substitute for anything else in life. She winked at him and walked to her bedroom on wobbly legs to change because she really did need to get some studying done.

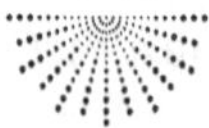

CHAPTER TEN

After grabbing some comfy clothes from her room, Syd went to the bathroom to clean up and change. And refocus her brain. If she could keep things simple with Hunter, she'd be fine. Sex was simple. It was pleasure, nothing more. But when he started digging into her life, things got complicated.

It wasn't that she had secrets. Sharing the personal stuff muddled any relationship. While she stepped into a pair of sweats, she made a mental list of safe topics for conversation. School worked, mostly because with the exception of getting her degree, school didn't matter all that much to her. Work was safe because no one wanted to hear her stories of her job in the campus bookstore. Music…Normally, she could discuss music with anyone because it became a discussion of likes and dislikes. However, with Hunter it evolved into explaining and understanding a shared passion. Could get sticky.

How could she avoid it, though? They were both on the marching band, she was filling in on the weekends, and she was teaching him to play drums. She supposed if she kept it surface-level stuff, it would be okay.

A knock on the bathroom door startled her. "You okay?"

"I'll be right out."

"Better hurry or there won't be any pizza left."

She swung the door open. "You just ate two sandwiches."

"Sex makes me hungry. Especially when I haven't had dinner. Gotta keep my energy up." A smile bloomed across his face that melted her.

She pushed past him to ignore what his smiles did to her. In the kitchen, she grabbed a plate and put two slices of slightly overdone pizza onto it. Hunter came up behind her and snagged a piece. His warm body crowded her, and she tried to muster the energy to be bothered, but in fact, she wanted to lean back into him.

"Mmm. Smells good." His nose pressed against the side of her neck, sending shivers through her.

She bumped her hips back to create space. "Did you find a movie to watch?"

"*Captain America.*"

"Really?"

"I live with a comic book artist. He makes me watch all the Marvel movies. I like this one."

"Whatever."

She carried her plate back to the living room and settled on the couch, pushing all thoughts of what they'd just done there out of her mind. Hunter sat next to her, shoving the last bit of crust into his mouth. The guy ate like a machine.

He put an arm around her shoulder so their

bodies touched from torso to calf. He was warm and solid and comfy enough to snuggle against, and she almost fell asleep.

Except he kept a running commentary going through the movie. It should've annoyed her, but he was funny. Near the end of the movie, Trish came home. She looked at them on the couch. One eyebrow shot up and she offered a stiff, "Hi."

After taking off her coat, she turned back to Sydney. "Can I see you a minute?"

Using Hunter's thigh to push up—she loved the muscle beneath her palm—she followed her sister into the kitchen.

In a harsh whisper, Trish said, "What are you doing?"

"Watching a movie. What's your problem?"

"I see what's going on." She pointed at the empty pan from the pizza and then back over Syd's face and body. "You stayed in." She lowered her voice even more. "And had sex."

"God. You're the one who told me to go out and have fun. I'm having fun."

"I wanted you to go on some dates, not fall into bed the first time you were alone with a guy."

"This isn't the first time we've been alone. It's no big deal."

Trish crossed her arms and stared.

"Don't worry. I have a couple of finals to take this week and then we're on break. Even I can't screw this up."

Trish huffed. "I worry about you."

"This isn't like Tony. Hunter's a senior. He'll probably get bored with me by the time break is over. I'm not giving him any power over me. I learned my lesson." At least she wanted to believe that.

"Be careful."

"Always."

"I'm going to bed."

Sydney got back to the living room just as the credits started to roll.

"You want me to rewind it? I didn't want to pause the movie because then it would seem like I was trying to listen."

"No. The movie was okay, but I don't need to see the end."

"Everything all right?"

"Yeah." She took her seat beside him, but he stood.

"I'm gonna go home."

Crap. He'd heard Trish. "You don't have to."

He smiled a goofy grin. "Yeah, I do. You said you had to study. I don't want you to be up all night because of me." He paused. "Well, yeah, I do, but not because you have to study. I want to keep you up doing other things."

She stood and grabbed his hand. "Other things sound good."

He bent and kissed her cheek. "Next week. After finals."

"Huh?"

"I'm leaving so you can study."

"Seriously?"

"Of course. I want you to do well. Maybe we can meet up for lunch or something tomorrow when you're ready for a study break."

She felt all warm and gooey inside. She'd given him an opening to have more sex, to spend the night, and he'd turned her down so she'd have time to study.

"What's that look?"

She didn't know what he saw on her face, but she smiled. "Nothing."

"You know I want to, right? I'm going to sleep tonight thinking about all the other things we can do, but I don't want to get in the way of your finals."

Double crap. Her throat tightened. He was not supposed to care about any of this. He was supposed to be a good-time guy.

"Call me if you need a break." He pulled away from her and went to the bedroom to get his shoes.

When he came back and put on his jacket, her throat was clear enough that she could speak. Instead, she chose to grab a handful of worn black leather and haul him in for a kiss. His arms came around her and her whole body hummed with pleasure. She swiped her tongue along his in a long slow glide.

She couldn't tell him how important it was to her that he wanted her to study, but she could show him how much she wanted him.

He suddenly gripped her hips, fingers squeezing a bit, and pushed her away. "I really need to go now."

His pupils were dilated so big that she could barely see the blue of his irises. He leaned in and pressed one more quick kiss to her lips. "Next weekend, you're all mine."

She liked the sound of that.

After he left, Sydney cleaned up a little and

turned off the TV. She was tired and relaxed, but she needed to study. If she left it until the last minute, she'd bomb the test. Her brain needed the slow build of information to retain it. It would help if it weren't so damn boring.

She opened up her notebook and the binder of handouts she'd received over the semester. Thirty minutes in, she was dozing.

Her phone buzzed on the table. Who the hell would call her this late?

A text from Hunter. **How's the studying?**

It sucks.

Why?

Too much information. Too many terms. Brain too tired. Then she snapped a photo of the papers spread all over the table and attached it.

Flashcards!

She stared at the word. The guy was crazy. What man ever used an exclamation point, especially in a text?

Before she could figure out how to respond, he sent another. **Seriously. By making the flashcards, you're reviewing the information. Then you can drill yourself for more practice. I know what I'm talking about. I'm a teacher. Almost.**

She laughed out loud with a snort. **What, am I in third grade?**

Trust me. I wouldn't steer you wrong. Now get back to work. We'll talk tomorrow.

Her stomach knotted. She already trusted him more than she had anyone in a long time. Part of her felt good, but mostly she was afraid of that trust. Trish was right to be worried. She had asked

Hunter to stay even though she was supposed to be studying.

And now, she was ignoring her notes to read texts from him. If he kept it up, she'd get nothing done. Lucky for her, he kept walking away. That back-and-forth was the biggest problem. She didn't know what to do with it.

He came on hot and heavy and left so she could study. Then he interrupted studying for what purpose? To make sure she was thinking about him? That had been Tony's signature move.

Of course Hunter had been all over her brain. He'd been all over her body and it was an experience she'd very much like to repeat. Lust often clouded her brain and her judgment.

Yet Hunter backed off without her having to remind him she had work to do. *He* reminded her. Was it possible that he was a good guy who cared?

She'd heard of such a species of man, although she'd never encountered one in the real world.

She had no idea what to do with him.

THE FOLLOWING MORNING, HUNTER GOT OUT OF bed with a smile on his face. He went to the kitchen wearing only his boxers. Adam was already there finishing a bowl of cereal.

"What are you doing up so early?" his roommate asked.

Hunter smiled.

"Are you sneaking out because you have a woman in your room? I am not playing go-between. There's nothing more awkward than having to explain to a stranger that her bed buddy took off."

"That only happened once. And there's no one in my bed." At least not yet. He'd love to get Sydney in his bed for an entire night.

"You're too happy *not* to have gotten laid."

"I never said I didn't get laid. I just said there wasn't a woman in my bed." He let Adam process that while he looked for coffee. The container was empty. "Fuck."

"You finished it."

He remembered now. He'd finished it off yesterday before going to the game. He'd meant to stop on the way home but forgot. "I'll grab some later."

"Get more cereal, too. We're running low."

That was one of the great things about living with his best friend. They didn't argue about stupid shit like groceries. If there was beer in the fridge and cereal in the cabinet, they were fine.

He really wanted coffee right now, though. Then inspiration hit. Since he'd have to go out for a cup of coffee anyway, he could bring one to Sydney. She'd been up late studying.

Adam stood and rinsed his bowl in the sink. "What the hell was that?"

"Huh?"

"You had this look like you were plotting to take over the world."

"No world domination for me." He patted Adam's shoulder on his way out of the room. He had a different plan in mind.

Less than an hour later, he was buzzing Sydney's door and hoped he wasn't waking up Trish.

Although the woman had seemed to like him fine when he arrived, her attitude had definitely shifted when she'd come home.

The outer door buzzed and he went through. When he got to the top of the stairs this time, though, Sydney wasn't waiting for him with an open door. Balancing both coffees and the bag of donuts in one hand, he knocked. He heard shuffling inside, waited a beat, and then put on his best smile for her to see through the peephole.

The door swung open and Sydney stared at him. She wore the same clothes he'd left her in last night and she looked sleep rumpled. "What are you doing here?"

"I ran out of coffee at home, so I had to go out to get some. Since I was out, I figured you might be ready for a study break." He held out a cup for her.

The look she offered was filled with suspicion, but she stepped aside to allow him to come in. Inside, he took in the mess of papers and books all over the table and floor. The picture she'd sent last night didn't do the disaster justice.

"I'm kind of afraid to ask how it's going."

"Still horrible. I tried to study, but just like in class, I kept falling asleep." She walked around him and sat on the couch, pulling her legs up in front of her. She sipped the coffee. "Thanks for this."

"I also brought donuts. Maybe not the breakfast of champions, but definitely the sustenance of crammers everywhere."

"I'm not cramming. At least I'm trying not to."

He shook off his coat and sat beside her. "How are you with your other classes?"

"Fine. It's just this one that's killing me."

He reached over and pulled out the pack of index cards he'd shoved in his jacket pocket.

She laughed. "Coffee, donuts, and index cards?"

"I know you think it's silly, but it can't hurt, right? It might even help. You won't fall asleep if you're writing notes on the cards."

She laughed so hard she had to put her coffee down. "You don't even know," she said unevenly. Then she handed him her notebook.

He flipped through the pages and saw what she meant. She'd been in the middle of writing something and the ink went off the page. She actually had fallen asleep while writing notes.

"You won't this time. I'll help."

"Don't you have your own finals to study for?"

"I have a paper to write and a history final. I've got it." He peeled back the plastic on the cards and handed her a small stack. "Start with relevant vocabulary words. Term on one side, definition on the other."

She sighed but accepted the cards.

As resistant as she was at the beginning, an hour and a half later Sydney had a pile of flashcards to study from and they'd spent most of that time laughing. While she finished up her last card, he straightened the mess of papers strewn around. He handed her the stack of cards.

"What's this?"

"Your flashcards."

She fanned them out like she didn't believe him. "We did all these?"

"*You* did them. I watched."

"Wow. I remember stuff."

"That happens when you stay awake."

Her face brightened with a sweet smile. He stood and looked around. He'd seen the entire apartment last night, except for Trish's room, but a thought occurred to him.

"Where are your drums?"

Her smile dropped and her mouth opened, then closed. "I don't have any right now."

"How do you practice?"

She lifted a shoulder. "School."

He couldn't imagine not having his instruments.

"Not all of us can tap parental guilt."

But she must've had a kit at some point. She danced along a line of answering his questions without revealing too much. "Why don't you have any right now? You used to have some."

She bit her lip. He could tell she was debating how much to say. "I sold them."

Her lips wobbled with the admission.

There was no way someone who loved to play as much as she did would've sold her drums. He sat down again and laid a hand on her leg. "Are you in trouble?"

She shook her head. "It was a long time ago."

The pain on her face still looked fresh. He ran his hand down to her knee.

"I don't want to talk about it."

He wanted to push. He wanted to know what could make her give up the one thing that was important to her. He'd seen her play through anger and frustration. She didn't have that outlet at home. It irritated him that she wouldn't open up.

"It's fine." She leaned forward and pressed her

lips to his. Rubbing her hands across his chest, she tried to push him back and climb onto him like she had last night. Although he'd thoroughly enjoyed the outcome then, he realized she used sex to avoid talking to him. Yesterday, she didn't want to talk about the trouble in biology. Today it was her drums.

He gripped her hips and set her back onto the couch.

"What?"

"Break's over. You have studying to do."

"I spent the last couple of hours working."

"And now you're set to review." He reluctantly stood and pulled on his jacket.

She had the same weepy look she gave him last night when he left.

"I'm not rejecting you, you know this, right?" He felt ridiculous saying it, but he needed to reassure her. He wasn't ready to walk away from what they had.

"Yeah," she said unconvincingly. She followed him to the door.

His good-bye kiss was more involved than he planned and they were both breathing erratically when he pulled away again. "After finals, I want a whole night with you. No jobs, no school, no tests. Just us naked and sweating and fucking all night."

Her breath shuddered out and she licked her lips. They were definitely on the same page. And then, when her defenses were down, he'd get her to spill her secrets.

The next few days both flew by and dragged. Sydney didn't see Hunter because of their school schedules and the end of football season. He texted her Monday night to ask how the biology final went—very well—but he made no move to see her. They skipped band practice on Tuesday night because everyone had finals. They still held Thursday's practice, and she assumed they'd do a drum lesson after. She'd missed hanging out with Hunter.

Jay and Lance had just left and Sydney sat behind the drums. "Ready for your lesson?"

He ran a hand through his hair and sighed. "As much as I'd love to, I have a paper I need to finish. It's due tomorrow and I got bogged down doing research. I need to take a rain check."

"Oh." She tried not to sound hurt, but she'd been looking forward to this for days. She'd missed his jokes and laughing with him and the heat of his body pressed against hers. He was only doing what she'd done this weekend, so it shouldn't bother her. "Okay. I'll get out of your hair then."

Damn, she sounded stupid. The guy just needed to finish his homework.

"I'd ask you to stay, but I wouldn't get any work done with you here."

She perked up. "Really?"

"Oh yeah." Then he grabbed her and kissed her breathless.

When he let her go, he whispered, "Tomorrow night after the gig. Can you spend the night? Or will Trish come looking for me?"

"Believe it or not, I'm an adult." The thought of spending a whole night with Hunter sent a shiver through her.

"I don't want to cause trouble between you and your sister, but I want you all night long. Maybe all day Saturday, too."

"That's a lot of time." Her voice was husky and she wanted to strip right there and let him get started.

"I have a lot of things I want to do. And I plan to take my time."

She nipped his bottom lip. "I look forward to it."

"Friday suddenly seems far away."

She chuckled.

"Are you free for lunch tomorrow?"

"Class gets out at eleven fifteen. Then I'm free till one." She kissed his jaw. "Will that be enough time?"

He groaned and stepped back. "Nope. I meant let's meet for lunch. Hang out. Bitch about our professors and the crappy classes we're happy to be done with."

"Like a date?"

"You kind of cheated me out of one last Saturday."

"I don't think that was cheating, but whatever."

"It was a hell of a way to spend my night, and I wouldn't have traded it for a dinner in a restaurant, but I want more than sex, Sydney. I want to get to know you better."

Huh. She rocked back on her heels. He kept knocking her off her game, and she wished she could tell what was genuine and what was his charm wheedling its way past her defenses. "You know me well enough."

Grabbing the waistband of her jeans, he hauled her back into him. A rush flooded through her veins. She expected a hot kiss, but he gently brushed his lips on her cheek, then her jaw, and finally her ear. "No. You hold back. I answer all your questions, but you brush mine off and distract me with sex."

He released his grip and she wobbled. Again, off balance. Every time she was alone with him. He was right, but she couldn't admit it. "I just want to get to the good stuff."

"You are the good stuff. But you still hold back."

She hated when he made her feel all warm and gooey.

"So about tomorrow?"

"I have to work. Help restock the bookstore for next quarter."

"Tomorrow night then." He gave her another quick kiss and shoved her through the door.

Sydney drove home with jittery emotions. Could she let Hunter in? What if telling him all about the real her—the one who let a guy take over her life—ruined everything between them? She wasn't sure if her greatest fear was that Hunter would be more like Tony or that he would look at her like she was a ridiculous mess.

On her way to bed, Trish stopped her. "How'd your finals go?"

"Good. Better than good, I think. Hunter helped."

Trish snickered. "Orgasm afterglow helped with the test?"

"Well, I definitely wasn't tense. But seriously, he came over on Sunday and helped me make flashcards. It worked."

"He was here on Sunday?"

Syd nodded. "He showed up with coffee and donuts while you were at the health club."

Trish narrowed her eyes.

Syd threw up her hands. "He helped me study. I offered sex and he turned me down. He told me to get to work, much like he did Saturday night when he left here."

Trish crossed her arms. "So he's putting school first? What kind of grades does he get?"

"How should I know? Good enough that he's graduating in May, which is on time, unlike me." She didn't want to be defensive, but she couldn't help it.

"Oh my God. You really like him. This isn't some quickie fling to get your feet wet."

"What are you talking about?"

"If you were just in it for the sex, you wouldn't be upset at my poking. You'd brush it aside. But you're sticking up for him."

"He's a good guy." She sincerely hoped she was right. Her guy picker didn't have a great track record.

Trish smiled, but said, "Remember to be careful."

"I am. I'm fine." Live carefully had become her life's motto. Hunter was making things harder than she was used to.

FRIDAY NIGHT, THE BAND PLAYED WITHOUT A HITCH. They played a double encore and Hunter would've played a third if it meant keeping the unabashed smile of pride on Sydney's face. After they loaded the van, they went back to the bar for a celebratory drink. Hunter stuck with water since he was driving, but encouraged Sydney to have a beer. Or two. He wanted her to relax because tonight was going to be all about them. Band was over, classes and finals were finished, so she had no more excuses. They could date and be a couple for the world to see.

He sat back on the stool and watched her get into a heated argument with Lance, of all people. Lance was probably the most laid-back guy he knew. In fact, Hunter couldn't remember Lance ever fighting with anyone about anything.

Whatever Sydney was trying to convince him of, however, she was animated about it. Her arms were waving and then she pointed, just short of poking Lance's chest. Then Lance doubled over in laughter. It was such a great sight to have his girlfriend blend with his lifetime friends.

He started at the words flowing through his head. *Girlfriend?* How the hell had that happened? He waited for panic to hit, but it didn't. He liked the idea. He'd dated a lot, but he rarely brought those girls around his friends. Some came to the shows at The Garage, but they acted like groupies, and while some guys might get off on that, he preferred someone to fit in.

Sydney definitely fit in.

Just then, she turned to him with a broad smile on her face. "Your friend Lance needs a brain transplant."

"Why's that?"

"He's trying to convince me the Stones had a greater impact on music history than the Beatles."

He shook his head, knowing better than to get involved in that argument. "You ready to go?"

Her cheeks grew pink and she looked at him from under her lashes. "Yeah."

He grabbed her hand and waved to the guys. "Did you tell Trish you won't be home tonight?"

She rolled her eyes. "It's fine."

He stopped walking and she crashed into him. "Uh-uh. Call her now or I take you home."

She released a long-suffering sigh.

"She'll worry about you."

"Fine." She pulled her phone out and texted Trish. As they headed toward the door, her phone rang. She answered as they got outside and Hunter ushered her to the van to keep warm.

"Hi, Trish." Then she listened. Hunter tried not to eavesdrop, but he couldn't help himself. "I'm fine. I'm staying with Hunter." Another minute of listening. "I will."

"Everything okay?"

"Yeah."

"If she's mad, I'll take you home."

"She's not mad. And she's not my mother. I can do whatever I want."

"But—"

"Nothing, Hunter. She worries about me, but she's not mad."

"If you're sure." He reached for her hand and interlaced his fingers. While they drove, she turned his radio up. He'd expected her to change the music, but she sat back with her eyes closed and listened to jazz.

With every passing moment with her, he liked her more. When he parked, she grabbed her back-pack and waited by the rear of the van.

"Come on," he said, pointing to the apartment.

"What about the equipment?"

"It'll be fine until morning. Adam will help me then."

"I can help."

He grabbed her hand and pulled her toward the house. "Maybe I can't wait."

He let them into the apartment and pulled her straight to his bedroom, where she dropped her bag.

"I know you're impatient and all, but I'd really like a shower."

"Let's go." He kicked off his shoes and stripped with her watching him.

"As much as I enjoy that sight, I'm not following. What if your roommate's here?"

"He's not."

"But he could come home." She toed off her shoes and slid them next to the wall.

Hunter led the way to the bathroom. He started the water and turned to Sydney. She reached for the hem of her tank top, but he stilled her hands. "Let me."

He removed her clothes, stopping to kiss her everywhere. By the time they stepped under the water, they were hotter than the spray. He held her close and ran his hands over her body, toying with her nipples, making her moan. Using his hands, he made her come the first time for the night.

Then they washed each other without talking. As they dried off, he watched her rub her skin with his towel. "You were really good tonight." Then he realized how that might've sounded, so he added, "At The Garage. You get off on performing, don't you?"

She dropped the towel and stepped close. She licked his ear before saying, "I get off on a lot of things."

"I'm going to see how many of those things I can hit."

"Ambitious, huh?"

"Determined." He backed her out the door. She squealed when the cold air of the hall hit them.

"I'm naked."

"I know."

She turned and bolted for his room. He followed at a slower pace, enjoying the display. When he closed the door and locked it, she was bent over digging through her bag.

"You won't need anything you have in there."

She stood, holding a huge T-shirt.

"Nope." He walked toward her, backing her to the bed. He didn't stop until she dropped the shirt and crawled backward onto his mattress. He started at her ankle and kissed his way up. As he neared her pussy, she spread her legs wide in invitation. He lay flat on his stomach and licked her. Flicking his tongue against her clit, he felt her thigh muscles jump in response.

He thrust his tongue inside her on a moan. Her taste and scent surrounded him and he would've died happy to drown in her. He kept stroking and sucking and lapping until her hips bucked up. Gripping tight and holding her to his mouth, he continued until her thighs trembled and she whimpered his name.

Rising up on his knees, he grinned at her.

"Don't look so smug."

"Can't help it." He kissed up her torso and spent a minute or two, maybe three, worshipping her nipples before reaching for a condom.

He eased into her slowly. Once he was settled inside her, she wrapped her arms and legs around him. They moved together in slow motion until the orgasms soared through them. This time it wasn't about getting to the finish line. He just wanted to be with her.

Lying together afterward, he thought about making his move, but she started the conversation first.

"What are you most worried about after graduation?"

"Getting a job."

Her fingers tapped against his ribs in a quiet rhythm. "Besides that. Everyone worries about a job."

He sighed, but if he wanted her to open up, he had to be willing to. "I'm afraid I won't be good enough. I worry that a student will ask something and I won't know the answer. I worry I'll get a boss who hates me. Or worse, doesn't take me seriously."

She didn't respond.

"My adviser warned me that I'm too friendly and some instructors I've worked with in the past aren't sure if I can hack it as a teacher."

"You'll be fine."

He snorted and she tilted her head up to face him. "You joke around a lot. You want people to like you. There's nothing wrong with that, but you know what to do when you have to be in charge."

"How would you know?"

"Why do you think you were chosen for section leader?"

He paused.

She splayed her hand on his chest, drumming a different beat. "It's because you're good. Players respect you. You know your shit, but you don't talk down to people. You're also the obvious leader of the band. Lance and Jay follow you. There's nothing wrong with enjoying what you do. Carry that into the classroom and not only will you be successful, but every kid will line up to take your class." She kissed his chest. "Especially the girls."

Of all the people he'd expected to give him a pep talk, he hadn't thought of her. After the serious ego boost, he was ready to understand her better. "Where were you before you transferred here?"

She turned her head to rest on his chest again, and when she spoke, her breath whispered across his skin. "I told you. I took some time off school. Did a year at community college."

"You actually didn't tell me anything. You always dodge. Why'd you take time off?"

She didn't answer and he wondered if she was trying to come up with a lie.

"I've told you everything. I talk about music and teaching. Hell, I even told you about Shelly." He traced her spine. "I want to know you."

"I don't want to tell you," she whispered. "It's embarrassing. I screwed up so bad."

"We all screw up."

"Not like this." She stroked his belly and played with the patch of hair on his chest. "In high school, I went out with a guy. His name was Tony. Star quarterback. Everyone loved him. But he chose me. We dated for two years. I was deep in love."

"Was he?"

"I think so. At least at first. He made me feel special. Like I was a prize. I hated the looks and comments I got from everyone else, though. No one understood how he could want me. But I sucked it up because he convinced me that none of them mattered. Only us."

She turned her head so she could prop it on

her hand. "And that's when the stupid took over. I wanted to go to New York for school. He was already accepted to Southern. He told me he couldn't go without me. He'd never make it. So I followed him to Carbondale."

Hunter's stomach sank. Somehow, he knew this was going to get bad. He clenched his jaw and waited for her to continue.

"Once we were there, things changed. He was even more of a star and he kept telling me he had an image to uphold, but he wanted me for himself. He didn't want to share me."

Crap. Hunter knew this story. This asshole was busy sharing himself. Still, Hunter said nothing. He just continued to caress her back.

"Everything was a party. Then he needed my help with his classwork, even if it meant mine suffered. I started missing class and failing. He didn't care." Her gaze held his, but her eyes filled.

"Then I found out about the other girls. The ones who fit his image better. I lost a year of college and I was broke and flunking. All I wanted was to go home. So I sold my drums to pay off my tuition balance and left."

Hunter's heart broke for her, but so much made sense now. Her reaction about missing class, not wanting band members to know about them, it all clicked.

"Tony was a prick."

She laughed and a tear leaked from her eye. Using the pad of his thumb, he brushed it away. "He didn't deserve you." His fingers found the dragon tattoo on her shoulder. "What's the story about this?"

She glanced at her shoulder as if she didn't know it was there. "I got a little rebellious after Tony. Defiant. Angry. So I did what everyone does when they act out. I got a tattoo."

"Why a dragon?"

"Dragons are known for their wisdom and the ability to see the big picture. They're fierce and strong." She licked her lips. "Everything I wanted to be. Everything I wasn't with Tony."

"I think you're wrong."

"About what?"

"You were always strong and fierce. Tony was just a prick."

"You said that already."

He rolled her over so he was on top, covering her body with his. "Don't hide from me anymore, okay? I couldn't watch you fall and not try to catch you. Trust me to not be like him."

Her vulnerability filled her face. She didn't speak, but she nodded.

As she did, he knew he was falling for her unlike any other woman he'd known.

CHAPTER TWELVE

For days after her late-night confessions to Hunter, Sydney suppressed her confused emotions. Hunter had asked her to trust him to be different from Tony. She already knew he was, but allowing him to see her ugly mistakes was scary, so she pushed the feelings away.

They slept together, played together, and hung out. Christmas came and went, and they did separate holidays. It was way too early for meeting family, so Syd was okay with a little distance there. Not having to worry about school or work helped. With the exception of Jay and Lance, though, she and Hunter were very much a couple alone. He still hadn't introduced her to his roommate or his other good friend Free. He talked about them often, but never suggested they get together.

Part of it felt like her early relationship with Tony. As if he didn't want others to know about her because she didn't fit his image. Part of her, maybe even most of her, knew it was bullshit. She was the one who insisted no one know about them and he was just following her rules, but that small part of her, that bit of complete insecurity, couldn't help but wonder.

Weeks ago he'd asked her to come to his New Year's Eve party, but he hadn't brought it up since. New Year's was this week.

They were having band practice on Monday night for a change because of the holiday. They practiced "Auld Lang Syne," but Sydney couldn't imagine anyone at The Garage wanting to hear it.

As they packed up, Lance said, "See you Thursday."

"I thought we weren't practicing because of New Year's Eve."

He looked at her like she was dense. "We're playing."

"What?"

"Fuck me. Hunter didn't tell you? He's having a party like he does every year. We're the entertainment."

"Oh." Her brain scrambled to make sense of why he wouldn't have mentioned it. Maybe Kevin was coming back from break early.

Lance shook his head, and when Hunter came back into the room, he said, "Great communication skills, dork."

"Huh?"

Lance shook his head again and left, which Sydney found funny. Lance didn't talk much, and after making a statement like that most people would've explained, but not Lance.

Hunter turned his attention to her.

"Lance just informed me that the band is the entertainment for your New Year's Eve party."

"Oh."

"Look, if Kevin's coming back and he wants to play, it's okay. You could've just said so."

Hunter scratched his head and then put his hands in his pockets. "Kevin's not back yet."

She said nothing. What could she say? He obviously had changed his mind about wanting her at the party.

"I was trying to figure out how to talk to you about it."

"Straight out is usually best."

"Usually, but last time I mentioned the party, you weren't too interested in coming."

She wanted to scream at him. Back then they were barely friends. Now they were sleeping together, in a relationship. At least that's what she thought.

He came close and held her hand. "I'd like you to be at the party, but it's going to be pretty packed." He filled his chest as if whatever was coming next would need lots of oxygen. "I'm not sure how many members of the marching band are coming. Last year, a whole lot did. I don't want you to be uncomfortable being here because of them. I made a promise to not let them know about us."

Oh, crap. This guy was so good at turning her into a puddle of goo.

He rubbed his thumb on the back of her hand. "If you don't want to come, no pressure."

She turned her body and tugged his hand to pull him closer. She released his hand and placed it on her hip before twining her arms around his neck. "I'd hate to lose my chance at a midnight kiss. Maybe we should practice."

So they did.

THE NIGHT OF THE PARTY HUNTER RAN BACK AND forth through the apartment filling up bowls with chips and stacking more plastic cups by the keg. Sydney had spent the night at home the previous night because he had to help Adam and Free get ready for the party. He wished she were here now, though.

Both Adam and Free swore they had dates, but Free was looking miserable, which was saying something because he was dressed as Doctor Who, his all-time-favorite character. That costume never failed to make him happy.

"Where's your date?" Hunter asked.

Free shrugged. "I don't know if she's coming. She wouldn't return any of my calls for the last few days."

Hunter almost questioned if Free had really asked her, but there was no way even Free could fake being that upset. "What did you do?"

"I have no fucking clue. I ran into her at my dad's holiday party. She came with her parents. She seemed really upset to find out I planned to work with my dad after graduation. She was under the impression that my goal was to be an actor."

"Didn't you ever talk about your major? Careers? Anything? That's like basic-level stuff."

"I don't know. She never asked, so I didn't offer. It's not like investment banking is an exciting topic for most people. If they don't ask, I don't mention it."

Hunter popped a tortilla chip into his mouth. "Let me guess. She saw the costumes and made the leap that acting is your passion."

"Not such a leap, but yeah. Looking back now, I can see where she made those assumptions and I didn't make the connection to correct her."

Hunter slapped a hand on his friend's shoulder. "Let me know if there's anything I can do to help. I hope she shows."

"'Hope is a dangerous thing. Hope can drive a man insane.'"

"I know it's sad when you pull out *The Shawshank Redemption*."

Free poured himself a beer and drank.

The apartment filled quickly, but it didn't get as crowded as last year. As people filed past him, he kept an eye out for Sydney. He greeted friends and pointed to the booze. About an hour in, Adam began drawing tattoos on guests and he thought of Sydney and her dragon. Maybe he should get a matching one for the night. He was thinking about where to have Adam draw it when a pair of feminine hands covered his eyes from behind.

The nails clicked and the cloud of perfume filling his airspace told him it wasn't Sydney. Instead of playing the silly guessing game, he peeled the fingers away and turned. Amy.

"Hi."

"You're supposed to guess before you turn around."

"What are you doing here?"

"I thought we could have a good night."

Whoa. "Sorry, Amy, but I'm seeing someone."

She laughed and looked around. "Yeah, okay."

"I'm serious."

She laughed harder. "We all know you don't do serious."

"You need to leave." He grabbed her elbow and turned toward the door. She yanked from his grasp.

"I'm not going anywhere, except to have a drink. If you don't want to hook up, I'm sure there are plenty of other single guys who will." She turned and sauntered off toward the kitchen.

His stomach sank, and then fell through the floor when he caught sight of Lisa walking his way. She greeted him with a kiss on the cheek before he could dodge it. When he asked her to leave, her response was similar to Amy's. At least when she walked away, she went in a different direction.

Ten minutes of avoiding all women had him sweating. Sydney still hadn't arrived and the band was supposed to start soon. He needed to talk to her before she ran into Amy or Lisa.

And just when he thought it couldn't get worse, someone punched his arm. He didn't have to turn to know it was Kelly.

Why the hell did the universe hate him?

She didn't offer any conversation. She simply said, "I'll catch you at midnight."

As much as he wanted to explain that no, she wouldn't, he knew it would be a waste of breath.

He did the next best thing: He went to his friends.

Free stood in front of a bowl of chips, staring

at them as if he had to make a decision about which one to eat.

"No sign of your girl yet?"

"Nope."

"I have a favor to ask."

Free straightened. The guy liked to have a mission.

"Amy, Lisa, and Kelly are all here."

"Ex-girlfriends?"

"Yeah, and they won't leave. My new girlfriend, Sydney, will be here soon. I don't want them to cause trouble. Last year was bad enough, and I didn't have a girlfriend then."

"You really like this girl."

Instead of shying away or dodging the truth, he simply said, "Yeah." Then he pointed out the three girls he desperately wanted to avoid.

Adam was no longer at his tattooing station, which was a small card table set up in the corner with a stash of markers sitting on it. Hunter wove through the crowd to find him.

Adam's bedroom was the last place he checked and where he found him drawing on Reese. "Here you are. A bunch of people are looking for you to tattoo them."

Adam shot him a look over his shoulder. "I'll be done in a minute."

Looked like Adam was interested in more than drawing a tattoo on Reese. Interesting. Hunter chuckled. "Maybe close and lock the door next time. Sock on the knob."

"Shut the hell up."

"For real, when are you going to be done? I need your help."

"Two minutes."

Hunter glanced over his shoulder and shuffled his feet.

Adam sighed. "Time me."

Hunter pulled out his phone and set the timer. Then he leaned against the wall beside the door so he could see if Sydney came in. Adam finished his drawing and he and Reese came out of the bedroom. "Hey, dude, can I talk to you?"

Adam told Reese where to get drinks and food. Then Hunter dragged him into the far corner of the living room. "I need your help."

"With what?"

"Amy, Lisa, and Kelly are all here."

"So?"

"I didn't invite them."

"Again, so?"

"I have a date planned for tonight. And it isn't any of them."

"These aren't the same girls from last year, are they?"

Hunter shook his head. Sure, he made jokes about the girls fighting last year, but it wasn't really funny. Especially now. "No, but they worry me."

Adam laughed. "What am I supposed to do about them?"

Biting back his irritation, he said, "Keep them away from Sydney. And me."

"First of all, who the hell is Sydney?"

"My date. She's our drummer for tonight."

How had Adam missed her being around?

Adam shook his head. "How do you suggest I keep them away?"

"Use your imagination. Tell them what a horrible guy I am. Introduce them to other guys. Tell them to leave. I don't care."

Adam stared at him. "Why not tell Sydney that these old girlfriends are here? I find being honest with a girl goes pretty far."

"Because she'll leave. She'll think I'm playing games and leave." The thought burned like acid in his stomach. He'd just gotten her to trust him and open up.

"Are you?"

"Playing games? No."

Adam agreed to do what he could and Hunter pointed out the girls to him as well. He looked around again. "Sydney should be here soon, so I'm going to go warm up."

"Did you try telling these girls you have a girlfriend? Maybe they'd take a hint."

"I tried. They laughed. Three conversations, three women, and they all thought I was kidding."

He could still hear their giggles, like he didn't even know how to have a serious conversation much less a relationship. No way could he let Sydney anywhere near them.

SYDNEY WALKED THROUGH THE UNLOCKED DOOR and into Hunter's crowded apartment. As she unwound her scarf, Hunter appeared out of nowhere.

"Hey," he said, tugging her elbow. "We're about to start playing."

She followed him, taking off her jacket as she

walked. "Sorry I'm late. Trish wanted to have a little drink and toast before I left since we won't be together at midnight. Traffic was a bitch, and I had to park, like, two blocks away. To top it off, I had to walk slow because half your neighbors didn't salt the ice and I didn't want to fall."

He gently shoved her toward the drums. "You want me to get you a drink?"

She shook her head. She'd never known him to rush anything. "I'm good."

"I need to talk to you."

"Okay." She sat behind the drums and pulled out her sticks. "Shoot."

He shot a glance over his shoulder. He opened his mouth, but Jay cut in. "You ready to start?"

Hunter nodded and grabbed his sax. They did a little warm-up, but were ready to jump right in. They played a couple of songs, but no one was dancing. It made her wonder why they didn't just turn on the radio. After a set, they took a break.

Hunter looked out over the crowd of people and took Sydney's hand. He pulled her through the apartment and straight to his bedroom. He shut the door and then closed in on her.

"What's going on?"

"Nothing. I missed you. And given your dislike of people knowing about us, I didn't want to do this in front of everyone." He held her hips to his and kissed her.

When he took it deeper, she was glad they were alone because his dick was prodding her stomach. "You told the band to take five. We don't have time for all that."

"I can't help what you do to me." He kissed her neck and ran his hands up the sides of her body.

She pulled away before they both lost control. She touched his face. "Everything okay?"

"Yeah. You want a drink or something?"

"You don't have to wait on me. I can get my own drink."

"I know. I should probably check on people and food and stuff. If you need anything, you can ask Adam or Free."

She chuckled. "I suppose I could if I knew who either of them were."

His eyes widened. "Uh, well, you can't miss Free. He's dressed like Doctor Who. Adam is the one drawing tattoos on people."

It wasn't quite an introduction to his friends, but it was better than nothing. "What did you want to talk about?"

"Huh?"

"When I first got here."

"Oh, that. Uh…" He got shifty and blew out a breath.

This wasn't the Hunter she was used to. No flirtation or quick smile here. "What's wrong?"

"There are a lot of people here—"

Syd's hand flew to his chest. "Don't worry about it. I know I told you I wanted us to be a secret, but I knew that people from marching band would be here. It's okay."

He opened his mouth to say something else, but she kissed him. "Let's get back to the party."

They left the bedroom and walked in opposite directions. Hunter was acting weird. Maybe it was because he had to play host and bandleader all at once. Maybe it was because this was the first time they'd be around other people as a couple. If anyone should be nervous it should be her.

She grabbed herself a crappy draft beer from the keg and a handful of chips. As she headed back to the living room, she spied the guy who had to be Free, but he was deep in conversation with a busty brunette in a clingy green dress. Although she saw people walking around with ink on their arms and hands, she didn't see anyone doing the actual drawing, so she didn't have any luck finding Adam.

Jay strummed his guitar to get everyone's attention. Syd made her way to the drums and set her beer on the windowsill behind her. Hunter stood next to her with his keyboard on a stand. With a quick smile for her, he counted for them to start.

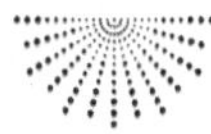

CHAPTER THIRTEEN

*B*urning seared through Sydney's arms. They'd played almost nonstop for hours. The party was in full swing and people had had enough alcohol that they were dancing like they would at a club. It gave her a rush of adrenaline like nothing else and propelled them all to keep playing.

It was nearing midnight and Sydney watched as couples paired off on the dance floor and in corners of the room. She wondered how many arrived as couples and how many jumped at the chance to be with someone for the night.

Hunter had no shortage of admirers as he played, but then again, so did Lance. She wasn't immune to the whole falling-for-a-rock-star thing, but she liked knowing that she'd be the one kissing Hunter at midnight.

As if he read her mind, he turned and winked at her. Then he called out to the crowd, "It's almost midnight." He pointed at her. "Drumroll, please."

She did the drumroll as the partiers did the

countdown. Noise erupted through the whole apartment. The band broke out in "Auld Lange Syne."

The drunks attempted to sing the words, but Sydney didn't think any of them had a clue as to what the lyrics actually were.

The band set down their instruments and the guys all did the man-hug with a "Happy New Year." Lance and Jay both gave her a real hug, but the only one she wanted to have her arms around was Hunter.

She walked around writhing bodies wondering where he'd taken off to, when a hand suddenly wrapped around her wrist. She spun to yell at the asshole for being grabby, but she faced Hunter and her anger melted away. "Been looking for you."

"Come here." He pulled her into his embrace. He cupped her jaw and their gazes locked.

"Hey, Hunter, I thought I was getting the midnight kiss."

He froze, his lips hovering over Sydney's. A look of fear came into his eyes. She could almost hear him thinking, "Busted."

Syd pulled away from him and turned to see who spoke. The girl was cute with long brown hair bouncing around her shoulders. She wore nothing fancy, just a Northwestern sweatshirt and jeans.

Behind her, a perky blonde smiled. "Is this the line to get a kiss from Hunter?"

Syd took another step back. She looked at the women and back at Hunter. A third one came up behind him and stroked a hand across his shoulder. It was a move she was obviously comfortable with. As she took in the scene, Sydney felt a whole new burn run through her.

Embarrassment. Foolishness. Heartbreak.

The night came into clear focus. Hunter had been acting weird because he hadn't wanted her here. He'd assumed she wouldn't come because of the band members who might see them together, so he'd invited other girls.

He kissed her hello in the privacy of his bedroom not because he wanted to be alone with her but because he didn't want the others to see.

She was such a fucking idiot.

She had no words. She was more upset with herself than anything. Shaking her head, she turned away. She grabbed her jacket from the floor near the drums and wove around couples oblivious to the pain she felt.

"Sydney, wait."

She didn't stop. What could he say? *I didn't mean to hurt you.* She didn't need the bullshit.

By the time she got to her car, tears streamed down her face. The cold wind whipped against her cheeks, threatening to freeze the tears in their tracks. Before her car was even warm, her phone started buzzing.

Hunter. She ignored the call.

She drove home in a daze and was glad to find Trish wasn't there. She couldn't talk. Not to anyone.

Her phone had gone off repeatedly since she'd left Hunter's, but he'd left only one message.

In the kitchen, she found a bottle of whiskey Trish kept for her boyfriend, and she slammed a shot. Then another.

Then she was ready to listen to Hunter's message. Between the tears and the alcohol, the buttons on her phone were blurry. After one failed attempt, she hit the right sequence to hear the message.

"Syd, please come back. I didn't invite these girls. I went out with them before, yeah, but I didn't ask them to come tonight. When I found them at the party, I asked them to leave. I told them I was with someone. They didn't take me seriously. Just like everyone else. Please. At least call me back so I know you're okay."

She threw her phone against the couch. No, she was not okay. She didn't know if she could believe anything he said. And what did that say about her and their relationship? She didn't want to be with a guy if this was going to be her reaction every time some woman talked to him. It would make her crazy.

But she wanted to believe him.

She closed her eyes and remembered the look on his face when they'd been interrupted. He'd been blindsided.

But he said nothing to tell them off. He didn't grab her and tell them she was his girlfriend. He'd said nothing.

His lack of response was pretty telling, too. She slugged back another shot and collapsed on the couch.

∼

HUNTER CAME BACK INSIDE FROM THE COLD. OF course Sydney didn't answer her phone. Why would she? She thought he was cheating on her. Anger surged through him as he walked back into the apartment. He needed to go after her, make her understand.

Inside, the party continued. No one took any notice of what had happened with Sydney. The three women who interrupted his midnight kiss were still standing in the middle of the living room.

He strode up to them and said, "Get out of my house and don't ever come back."

Amy looked up at him with wide eyes. "What did we do?"

He threw up his hands. "I told you all when you got here I was off the market, that I was seeing someone. None of you took me seriously. Listen to me now." He made eye contact with each of them. "The best thing that ever happened to me just walked out the door because of your stupid games. I don't ever want to see any of you again."

Kelly spoke up. "Damn. You're serious." She turned to the other two. "Guess we didn't have it, girls. Let's leave him."

Together they walked away as if they hadn't just destroyed his relationship. He made his way through the apartment looking for Free or Adam to tell them he was leaving. He couldn't find either of them. He glanced around. Would anyone notice if he took off, too?

He grabbed Mike from marching band, who at least looked kind of sober. "I have to leave. If you see my roommate, let him know I'll be back later."

"Will do. Great party, by the way. Lots of single

women. I don't know how you do it, but I'm grateful."

Hunter slapped Mike's shoulder. "Enjoy yourself. They're all yours."

And he meant it. No one else could capture an ounce of his attention. As he put on his jacket, he tried to think about what he would say to Sydney to convince her that she was the only one for him. He saw his sax sitting by the window where less than an hour ago he'd played side by side with Sydney.

He grabbed it, thinking he might need all the help he could get, and left his own party.

He parked in front of Sydney's apartment and called her again. She still wouldn't pick up, but he knew she was home because her car was parked behind him. He got out and rang the bell. Still no answer.

Back in his van, he sat rubbing his hands together to keep warm. He eyed his sax. If she wouldn't listen to words, maybe she'd listen to music. He climbed out and stood on the frozen sidewalk.

He played the one song he needed her to hear: "Have a Little Faith in Me."

~

"WHAT IS THAT?" TRISH ASKED FROM THE KITCHEN.

"What?"

"That music."

Sydney shrugged. "It's New Year's. Everyone's loud."

"Uh-uh." Trish crossed the room and looked out the window. "Oh my God. It's Hunter."

"Damn him." Sydney's head was even fuzzier than it had been a half hour ago even though she'd stopped drinking. When Trish came home, she gave her the abridged version of the story. "I thought he left when I didn't answer the door."

"Honey, if you want to pretend to not be home, it's not a good idea to park your car in front of your house."

"I'm not pretending anything." Her heart hiccupped because she hadn't faked any of it with Hunter. "I don't want to see him."

Trish stood, holding the curtain aside. "What song is that?"

Syd closed her eyes and listened. It didn't take long for her to recognize it. With recognition came a fresh bout of tears. "'Have a Little Faith in Me.'"

"The dude's gotta be freezing out there. It takes guts to not only come after you but to stand out there and play solo."

"Putting on a performance is no big deal for him."

"But this one's for you."

Syd brushed away the tears.

"I'm letting him in." Trish opened the window and yelled, "I'm buzzing you up."

"No," Sydney said.

Trish went to the buzzer and pressed the button. "You need to talk to him. Even if it's just to say fuck you. Plus, our neighbors are going to start getting annoyed."

A soft knock sounded on the door.

"Do you want me to stay?"

Syd shook her head. Trish was right. She needed to do this.

Trish opened the door, offered Hunter a small smile, and said, "Good song." Then she went to her room.

Hunter closed the door behind him but didn't come all the way into the apartment. Sydney stared at him. For a change, he was hard to read. He looked miserable, but angry and defiant, like he was ready for a fight.

Too bad she wasn't.

He took a couple of steps forward and set his sax on the chair. He took off his jacket and laid it over the sax. Then he sat beside her on the couch, careful not to touch her.

All she wanted was to curl into him and that made her mad all over. She was so damn weak.

"Thanks for letting me in."

She snorted.

"I know it was Trish, but you didn't stop her." He ran a hand through his hair. "Look, I knew those girls. I'm not going to lie. I dated all of them. But I didn't invite them to the party."

"I heard your message." Her voice was scratchy from crying and a lump was still lodged in her throat, making talking painful.

"Do you believe me?"

She nodded.

"Then why are you crying?"

She swallowed and pushed words past the lump. "Because this can't work."

"What?" He moved closer and touched her thigh.

His fingers were frozen and she felt the cold through her jeans.

"Even if I believe you weren't doing anything with those girls, how can we have a relationship if that's what I think of you?"

He held her hand and she wanted to cry again. She stared at the way his fingers slid into hers.

"Sydney, look at me."

She did.

"I haven't lied to you about anything. I should've told you about those girls as soon as you showed up. I was going to tell you. When you first came to the house and when we were alone in the bedroom. But I chickened out. I knew you'd get mad and probably leave. I thought I could just keep them away from us and everything would be okay." He licked his lips.

"So you were trying to protect me?"

"No. I was protecting me. And us. I didn't want anything to mess with us because I love what we are together."

"We're a mess."

"A little, maybe. I want that mess with you."

"You'll get tired of my insecurities, my getting jealous when I see you with another girl, my fear of what people will say about me when they see us together."

He lifted her hand to his mouth and kissed it. "They won't be saying anything about you. They'll look at me and say, 'How the hell did he get a woman like that?'"

She laughed. He always knew how to make her feel better.

"I'm falling for you, Syd, and it'd be a terrible waste to walk away from that."

"You're falling—"

He nodded. "In fact, I think I already fell. Don't give up on us."

"Have a little faith?"

He nodded and cupped her jaw. "I have enough to share." He covered her mouth with his. His lips were cold, but his tongue hot.

Kissing him brought all of her emotions swimming to the surface. His kissed her like he played his music, holding nothing back, and he made her want to do the same.

She wanted to absorb everything he offered: his faith in them, his love.

He pulled back for a breath and leaned his forehead against hers. "Are you in?"

"All in."

His lips met hers again. His kiss muddled her brain more than any amount of alcohol, but it filled her heart with happiness. Yeah, they definitely had a shot.

If you liked *His New Jam*, don't miss *His Work of Art* and keep reading for a sneak peek of *His Dream Role*! If you have a moment and could write a brief review of this book, I would appreciate it.

You can sign up for my newsletter and get a free epilogue to read what our nerds are up to after college.

Be sure to also check out the first Hot & Nerdy trilogy as well as Shannyn Schroeder's contemporary romance series, The O'Learys:

More Than This
A Good Time
Something to Prove
Catch Your Breath
Just a Taste
Hold Me Close

HIS DREAM ROLE

*J*ust as Free Mitchell parked his car at the health club, his phone started buzzing with a text. He should've called Cary as soon as he'd known he'd be late.

Are you coming?

Parking now.

Free ran around to the front of the building, where he knew he'd find his brother waiting outside. Even after all these months, Cary still wouldn't go in without him.

"Sorry I'm late. You could've started without me. It's not like you need me there anymore."

"I know. I like the company. So what made you late?"

"I was with Hunter and Adam talking about the New Year's Eve party."

"Let me guess—you had to wait on Hunter."

"Of course." Free reached over and pulled the door open.

As he walked through, Cary asked, "How'd it go?"

"The usual. Hunter wants a big blowout like

last year, but Adam and I don't. Hunter said he'd limit his invites if Adam and I have dates."

Cary laughed. Like out-loud-drawing-attention laughter.

"It's not that funny," Free said as they entered the locker room.

"You haven't had a girlfriend since last spring."

Free couldn't argue because his brother would know if he lied. He hadn't even had a real date since Kim broke up with him. He blamed being out of practice; he and Kim had dated for over a year. In reality, he sucked at asking girls out.

Cary changed quickly while Free waited. He never did a real workout with Cary. He was there just for the wow factor. As Cary grabbed a towel, Free adjusted the lapels on his coat and straightened his earflap hat. Showtime.

Some costumes he wore required more props. Sherlock Holmes was simple. Unfortunately, many people didn't necessarily get it, even with the overcoat and hat, so he carried an oversized magnifying glass with him to aid in his sleuthing.

Truth be told, Cary no longer needed his help. Last summer, after the doctor told Cary he absolutely had to get off his fat ass and lose weight, Free offered to work out with him. Cary admitted that it wasn't the working out that bothered him as much as the people staring at him.

So three days a week for the past six months or so, Free dressed in outlandish costumes to draw attention away from his overweight brother.

Cary sat down at the first machine to work his legs and Free leaned against the adjacent machine.

For a change, the room wasn't crowded and no one took notice of them.

"What are you going to do about Hunter?"

Cary talking to him during the workout was a relatively new development. For months, they walked in together, but Free would stroll through the gym drawing attention to himself in subtle ways. Over the last month or so, they'd spent more time hanging out during Cary's workout. Soon, Cary wouldn't need him to show up at all.

"I'm going to prove him wrong. I'll find a date for the party."

Cary extended his legs and brought them back. "See if she has a sister, okay?"

The workout routine continued on in the same manner, Cary working various muscle groups and chatting. They talked about work and the holidays and Free soon became bored.

When Cary got on the treadmill, Free wandered around, trying to find something of interest. Two muscle-bound guys came out of the locker room and sneered at him.

One said, "Who do you think you are?"

Channeling the arrogance of his father, as he did every time he needed to portray Holmes, he answered, *"I'm a high-functioning sociopath. Sher-*lock Holmes."

He cocked an eyebrow and waited for them to respond. The first guy elbowed the other and they called a few friends over.

A ball of nerves plummeted through Free. He'd never been much of a fighter and he knew he couldn't hold his own with the first two, much less all their friends. He looked at the group and said in his best British accent, "*I dislike being outnum-bered. It makes for too much stupid in the room.*"

To his surprise, all the guys started to laugh. Sure, he was insulting them, and he was pretty sure they understood that, but they still laughed. Free pulled out his magnifying glass, nodded to them, and walked back toward the treadmills.

Cary slowed his pace. "Problem?" he asked, tilting his chin toward where Free had come from.

"Nope. Just my winning personality creating more fans." He leaned against the rail of the tread-mill while Cary jogged and watched the TV in front of them. Cary had it tuned to the financial reports. Free didn't need to hear the anchor or have closed-captioning on. He simply watched the numbers scrolling at the bottom of the screen. The red and green digits soothed him like a lullaby would a baby.

When Cary stepped off the treadmill, Free fol-lowed him to the locker room. "I'm going so I'm not late for rehearsal, okay?"

"Sure. See you later."

He walked out the front door of the health club, but instead of heading to the parking garage around back, he went to the coffee shop down the street. For the last month, there was a woman who came in at the same time he did. Samantha—he loved places that made it easy to learn everyone's name. In light of Hunter's challenge to get a date, and Cary's laughter at the thought, Free decided that today would be the day he would speak to her.

He entered the shop and a warm blast of air hit him. The shop wasn't usually busy at this time and today was no different. As he approached the counter, Samantha was in front of him, digging through her purse. The cashier watched her with impatience just short of rolling her eyes.

"I'm so sorry. I know I had cash in here." Her long, light brown hair created a curtain across her cheek. "I can't believe they stole it again."

For a change things actually worked in Free's favor. He wouldn't need to force an introduction. He pulled out money and said, "Here. Let me."

The cashier smiled brightly at him. "Anything for you?"

"Large black. Thank you."

She charged him for both coffees and Samantha stared at him with her wide, pink-lipped mouth hanging open. He had the sudden urge to feel those lips against his.

"Thank you," she finally managed. "I can pay you back."

"No big deal."

From the other side of the counter, the barista called, "Samantha."

Free pointed over his shoulder. "Your coffee's ready."

She took a step, then paused. "How did you know?"

He winked at her. "Elementary, my dear. I'm here at this time three days a week. They call your name every time."

"Hey, Sherlock." The barista thought he was funny.

Free followed Samantha to the other end of the counter and grabbed his cup.

Samantha smiled. Her whole face brightened

as she looked up at him, her amber eyes shining, and said, "Thanks again. I appreciate it. I'll get yours next time I see you."

"Until then." He gave her a tip of his hat and turned to leave. If he had his way, he'd be sharing a cup of coffee with her by week's end.

As the bizarre Sherlock Holmes pushed the door open and held it for an elderly couple, Sam surreptitiously snapped a photo on her phone. She sat at a table and texted her best friend, Jess. **Guess who just bought me a cup of coffee? Sherlock.**

A minute later, her phone rang. "Hey, Jess."

"Where do you find the weirdos?"

"I'm at the same place I always get my coffee."

"And Sherlock Holmes just walked in and bought you a cup of coffee."

"My ten bucks was stolen out of my purse again." As soon as the words left her mouth, she wanted to yank them back because Jess was going to start yelling.

"Jeez, Sam, we talked about this. When you're at the shelter, you need to lock up your shit. I get that you want to help people, but that doesn't mean they won't steal from you."

Sam sighed. She did know better. She'd mostly learned her lesson her first week when her whole purse went missing. Now she only carried a small amount of cash on her, and bottom line, she figured if a kid stole it, he needed it more than she did. "I know," she finally huffed back. "Anyway,

Sherlock came up behind me and paid for my coffee."

She took a sip and waited for Jess's reaction.

"So, does he think he's really Sherlock?"

"Hmm…I don't think so. I've seen him in here before. He's always dressed weird, like in costume. Once he was Riddler and another time, a Jedi? And then again the guy with the pointy ears from the other show."

"So he's a supreme weirdo."

Sam smiled. "He was nice. He bought my coffee and left. He's cute."

"Oh God. Please tell me you didn't give him your phone number or make plans for a date."

"Nope." She knew better than to tell Jess that she planned to buy him a coffee as a thank-you. Jess might be right. He could be a total weirdo. In fact, the first few times she saw him, she was concerned that he might have some mental issues. But his costumes were too well crafted and he functioned well in public, so she figured he was just eccentric.

"I mean it, Sam. Find a normal guy."

Sam choked on her coffee. After clearing her throat and regaining the ability to breathe, she said, "I date normal guys."

"You intentionally find strange ones just to piss off your dad. You're getting a little old for that."

"Whatever. I gotta go. Talk to you soon." She disconnected quickly because Jess had known her long enough to know that was exactly what she'd done for years. Her dad had an idea of the kind of guy he wanted Sam to be with, so Sam rebelled. However, Sam really did like the guys she picked.

At first. She tended to fall hard and fast. It was her nature.

Sherlock was different. He was far from a bad boy. Maybe sweet and quirky was her type. Everyone had a type, right?

She finished her coffee, tossed the cup, and bundled up for the cold. As she exited the shop, she looked toward her car and wished she could abandon it. The Mercedes made her stick out everywhere she went. She believed the damn thing was the reason kids at the shelter were okay with stealing from her. The car screamed *I'm rich!*—which she wasn't. Her parents were well off, not her.

The car had been her compromise. She'd wanted to live in the city to be closer to the locations where she would work and where she currently volunteered. Her parents flipped. They couldn't have their baby living in unsafe situations and—gasp—taking public transportation.

They ultimately came to a compromise on an apartment and Sam agreed she'd use the car to get to and from classes and her volunteer work. When she'd agreed, however, she'd imagined a regular car, like a Civic or RAV4. Her dad's compromise was getting a low-end Mercedes, as if one actually existed.

She pressed the key fob to disarm the car and got in. Admittedly, she did enjoy the heated seats when the weather turned. That probably made her a hypocrite.

The problem was, she wasn't quite sure who she was supposed to be yet and graduation was looming. Part of her wanted to continue on for her master's degree immediately so she could stay in her safe cocoon of school, where she knew exactly who she was. A bigger part of her, though, loved the work she did at the shelter, and she felt like she belonged there, like she made a difference.

She had a hard time reconciling the Mercedes-driving, heated-leather-seats Sam with the woman who wore yoga pants splattered with finger paint.

Sam pulled into her parking spot in the lot behind her apartment and sat in her car for a minute. A nagging feeling had been gnawing at her for months. Her life felt unsettled in a way it never had before. Jess's point about her dating habits hit home. She needed to decide what she really wanted and why.

The problem with that was she was going to a school, driving a car, and living in an apartment her father paid for. If she took the stand that she wanted independence, was she willing to walk away from everything that made her life comfortable?

Hot & Nerdy

Her Best Shot

Her Perfect Game

Her Winning Formula

His Work of Art

His New Jam

His Dream Role

O'Learys

More Than This

A Good Time

Something to Prove

Catch Your Breath

Just a Taste

Hold Me Close

For Your Love

Under Your Skin

In Your Arms

Through Your Eyes

From Your Heart

Stand Alones

Between Love and Loyalty

Meeting His Match

<u>**Daring Divorcees Series**</u>

One Night with a Millionaire

My Best Friend's Ex

My Forever Plus-One